THE CAMPFIRE GIRLS
SERIES

ॐ

The motor boat kept dashing back and forth,
making swimming almost impossible.

A Campfire Girl's Adventure

By
JANE L. STEWART

CAMPFIRE GIRLS SERIES
VOLUME IV

WILDSIDE PRESS

The Camp Fire Girls In the Mountains

CHAPTER I

PEACEFUL DAYS

On the shores of Long Lake the dozen girls who made up the Manasquan Camp Fire of the Camp Fire Girls of America were busily engaged in preparing for a friendly contest and matching of skill that had caused the greatest excitement among the girls ever since they had learned that it was to take place.

For the first time since the organization of the Camp Fire under the guardianship of Miss Eleanor Mercer, the girls were living with no aid but their own. They did all the work of the camp; even the rough work, which, in any previous camping expedition of more than one or two days, men had done for them. For Miss Mercer, the Guard-

ian, felt that one of the great purposes of the
Camp Fire movement was to prove that girls and
women could be independent of men when the
need came.

It was her idea that before the coming of the
Camp Fire idea girls had been too willing to look
to their brothers and their other men folks for
services which they should be able, in case of
need, to perform for themselves, and that, as a
consequence, when suddenly deprived of the sup-
port of their natural helpers and protectors, many
girls were in a particularly helpless and unfortu-
nate position. So the Camp Fire movement, de-
signed to give girls self-reliance and the ability
to do without outside help, struck her as an ideal
means of correcting what she regarded as faults
in the modern methods of educating women.

Before the camp on Long Lake was broken up
they hoped to have a ceremonial camp fire, but
there were gatherings almost every night around
the big fire that was not a luxury and an orna-
ment at Long Lake, but a sheer necessity, since

the nights were cool, and at times chilly. This fire was never allowed to go out, but burned night and day, although, of course, it reached its full height and beauty after dark, when the flames shot up high and sent grotesque shadows dancing under and among the trees, and on the sandy beach which had been selected as the ideal location for the camp.

At these meetings everyone had a chance to speak. Miss Eleanor, or Wanaka, as she was called in the ceremonial meetings, did not attempt to control the talk on these occasions. She only led it and tried, at times, to guide it into some particular channel. It would have been easy for her to impress her own personality on the girls in her charge, since they not only admired, but loved her, but she preferred the expression of their own thoughts, and she knew, also, that to accomplish her own purpose and that of the founders of the Camp Fire, it was necessary for the girls to develop along their own lines, so that when they reached maturity they would have formed the habit of thinking things out for themselves and knowing the reason for things, as well as the facts concerned.

"I think we're too likely to forget the old days when this country was being explored and opened up," Eleanor said one night. "Out west that isn't so, and out there, if you notice, women play a much bigger part than they do here. Those states in the far west, across the Mississippi, give women the right to vote as soon as women show that they want it. They are more ready to do that than the states in the east."

"Why is that, Wanaka?" asked Margery Burton, one of the Fire-Makers of the Camp Fire.

"In the west," said Eleanor, answering the question, "men and women both find it easier to remember the old days of the pioneers, when the women did so much to make the building of our new country possible. They faced the hardships with the men. They did their share of the work. They travelled across the desert with them, and, often, when the Indians made attacks, the women used guns with the men.''

''But there isn't any chance for women to do that sort of thing now,'' said Dolly Ransom, or Kiama, as she was known in the ceremonial meetings. ''The Indians don't fight, and the pioneer days are all over.''

''They'll never be over until this country is a perfect place to live in, Dolly, and it isn't—not yet. Some people are rich, and some are poor, and I'm afraid it will always be that way, because it has always been so. But everyone ought to have a chance to rise, no matter how poor his or her parents are. That was the idea this country was built on. You know the words of the Declaration of Independence, don't you? That all men are created free and equal? This was the first country to proclaim that.''

''But what is there to do about that?''

''Ever so many things, Dolly. Some men who have money use it to get power they shouldn't have, to make people work without proper conditions, and for too little money. Oh, there are all sorts of things to be made right! And one reason that some of them have gone wrong is that women who have plenty of comforts, and people to look after them, have forgotten about the others. There is as much work for women to do now as there ever was in the pioneer days— more, I think.''

''The Camp Fire Girls are going to try to make things better, aren't they, Wanaka?'' asked Margery Burton. For once she wasn't laughing, so that her ceremonial name of Minnehaha might not have seemed appropriate. But as a rule she was always happy and smiling, and the name was really the best she could have chosen for herself.

''Yes, indeed,'' said Eleanor. ''So far we've been pretty busy thinking about ourselves, and doing things for ourselves, but there has been a reason for that.''

''What reason, Miss Eleanor?'' asked Dolly.

''Well, it's hard to get much done unless you're in the right condition to do it. You know when an athlete is going to run in a long race, he doesn't just go out and run. He trains for it a long time before he is to run, and gets his body in fine condition. And it's the same with a man who has some mental task. If he has to pass an examination, for instance, he studies and prepares his mind. That's what we have to do; prepare our minds and bodies. In the city, in the winter, we will take up a lot of these things. I'm just mentioning them to you now so that you can think about them and won't be surprised when we start to go into them seriously.''

"I know something I've thought about myself,'' said Dolly, eagerly. "In some of the stores at home they have seats so that the girls can sit down when they don't have to wait on people. And in some they don't. But in the stores where they do have them, the girls get more done, and one of them told me once that she felt ever so much stronger and better when the rush came in the afternoon, if she'd been able to sit down instead of standing up all day.''

4—C 2

"Of course. And that's a splendid idea, Dolly. Some of the stores make the girls stand up all day long, because they think it pleases the women who come in to shop. But if you could make those store keepers see that they'd really get more work done by the girls if they let them rest when the stores are empty, they'd soon provide the chairs, even if the law didn't make them do it."

"This place looks as if pioneers might have lived here, Wanaka," said Margery Burton.

"They passed along here once, Margery, years and years ago, but they were going on, and they didn't stop. You see, the reason this country has stayed so wild is that it's hard to get at. The trees haven't been cleared away, and roads haven't been built."

"Isn't it good land? Wouldn't it pay to plough it, after the trees were cut down?" asked Bessie King.

"It would, and it wouldn't, Bessie. It's just about the same sort of land as in the valleys below, where there are some of the best farms in the whole state. But we need the forests, too. You know why, don't you?"

"No, I don't," said Bessie, after a moment's thought. "I know they're beautiful, and that it's splendid for people to be able to come up here and live, and camp out. But that isn't the only reason, is it?"

"No, it isn't even anywhere near the most important, Bessie. You know what a dry summer means, don't you? You lived long enough on Paw Hoover's farm at Hedgeville to know that?"

"Yes, indeed! It's bad for the crops; they all get burned up. We had a drought two or three years ago. It never rained at all, except for little showers that didn't do any good, all through July and August, and for most of June, as well. Paw Hoover was all broken up about it. He said one or two more summers like that would put him in the poor-house."

"Well, if there weren't any forests, all our summers would be like that. The woods are great storehouses of moisture, and they have a lot to do with the rain. Countries where they don't have forests, like Australia, are very dry. And that's the reason.''

''They have something to do with floods, too, don't they, Wanaka?'' asked Dolly. ''I think I read something like that, or heard someone say so.''

''They certainly have. In winter it rains a good deal, and snows, and if there are great stretches of woods, the trees store up all that moisture. But if there are no trees, it all comes down at once, in the spring, and that's one of the chief reasons for those terrible floods and freshets that do so much damage, and kill so many people.''

''But if that's so, why are the trees cut down so often?''

''That's just one of the things I was talking about. Some men are selfish, you see. They buy the land and the trees, and they never think, or seem to care, how other people are affected when they start cutting. They say it's their land, and their timber; that they paid for it."

"Well, I suppose it is—"

"Yes, but like most selfish people, they are short-sighted. It is very easy to cut timber so that no harm is done, and in some countries that really are as free and progressive as ours, things are managed much better. We waste a whole forest and leave the land bare and full of stumps. Then, you see, it isn't any use as a storehouse for moisture, which nature intended it to be, and neither is it any use to the timber cutters, so that they have to move on somewhere else."

"Could they manage that differently?"

"Yes, if they would only cut a certain number of trees in any particular part of the woods in any one year, and would always plant new ones for every one that is taken out, there wouldn't be such a dreadful waste, and the forests would keep on growing. That's the way it is usually done abroad—in Germany, and in Russia, and places like that. Over there they make ever so

much more money than we do out of forests, because they have studied them, and know just how
everything ought to be done."

"Don't we do anything like that at all?"

"Yes, we're beginning to now. The United States
government, and a good many of the states, have
seemed to wake up in the last few years to the
need of looking after the woods better, and so
I really believe that in the future things will be
managed much better. But there has been a terrible lot of waste, here and in Canada, that it
will take years to repair."

"They don't spoil the woods about here that
way, do they?"

"No; but then, you see, this is a private preserve, and one of the reasons it is so well looked
after is that some of the men who own it like
to come here for the shooting."

"I know," said Margery. "I thought that was
why the guides were kept here."

"It is, but it's only one reason. A few miles
away, if we go that way, I can show you acres

and acres of woods that were burned two years
ago, and you never saw such a desolate spot in
all your life. It's beginning to look a little better
now, because, if you give nature a chance, she
will always repair the damage that men do from
carelessness, and from not knowing any better.''

''Oh, I think it would be dreadful for all these
lovely woods to be burned up! And that wouldn't
do anyone any good, would it?''

''Of course not! That's the pitiful part of it.
But a terrible lot of fires do start in the woods
almost every year. You see, after a hot, dry
summer, when there hasn't been much rain, the
woods catch fire easily, and a small fire, if it isn't
stamped out at once, grows and spreads very fast,
so that it soon gets to be almost impossible to put
out at all.''

''I saw a forest fire once, in the distance,''
said Dolly. ''It was when I was out west, and
it looked as if the whole world was burning up.''

''I expect it did, Dolly. And if you'd been
closer, you'd have seen how hard the rangers and

everyone in the neighboring towns had to fight
to get control of that fire. It doesn't seem as
if they could burn as fast as they do, but they're
terrible. It's the hardest fire of all to put out,
if it once gets away. That's why we have such
strict rules about never leaving a camping place
without putting out a fire.''

''Would one of the little fires we make when
we stop on the trail for lunch start a great big
blaze?''

''It certainly would. It's happened just that
way lots and lots of times. Many campers are
careless, and don't seem to realize that a very
few sparks will be enough to start the dry leaves
burning. Sometimes people see that their fire
is just going out, as they think, and they don't
feel that it's necessary to pour water on it and
make sure that it's really dead. You see, the
fire stays in the embers of a wood fire a long,
long time, smouldering, after it seems to be out,
and then—well, can't you guess what might
happen?''

"I suppose the wind might come up, and start sparks flying?"

"That's exactly what does happen. Why, in the big forest preserves out west they have men in little watch-towers on the high spots in the hills, who don't do anything but look for smoke and signs of a fire. They have big telescopes, and when they see anything suspicious they make signals from one tower to the next, and tell where the fire is. Then all the rangers and watchers run for the fire, and sometimes, if it's been seen soon enough, they can put it out before it gets to be really dangerous."

"Well, I know now why I've got to be careful," said Dolly. "I wouldn't start a fire for anything!"

"Good! And I think it's time to sing the good-night song!"

CHAPTER II

"I think we'll beat those old Boy Scouts easily when we have that field day, Bessie," said Dolly Ransom to her chum, Bessie King. "Look at the way we beat them in the swimming match the other day."

A friendly rivalry between the Camp Fire Girls and the Boy Scouts of a troop that was camping at a lake some miles away had led, a short time before, to a swimming contest in which skill, and not speed and strength, had been the determining factors, and, vastly to the surprise and disgust of the boys, the girls had had the best of them.

"We don't want to be over-confident," said Bessie. "You know they thought we were easy, and I don't believe they tried as hard as they might have done. After all, girls and boys aren't

27

the same, and if boys are any good, they're
stronger and better at games than girls, no matter how good the girls are."

"Oh, they tried right enough," said Dolly.
"They just couldn't do it, that's all."

"Another thing, Dolly, we've got to remember,
is that those weren't races. If they had been
we'd have been beaten, because those boys could
really swim a lot faster than we could. It was
just a case of doing certain things and doing
them just the right way. Anyone can learn that
if they're patient enough, and it's not really very
important. I'm glad we won, because I think
boys sometimes get the idea that girls can't do
anything, and it's just as well for them to find
out that we can."

"You're getting on, Bessie. When you first
came from Hedgeville you wouldn't have believed
that, or, if you had, you wouldn't have said it."

"Oh, I think I would have, Dolly. You know
about the only boy I had much to do with in those
days was Jake Hoover, and you saw him when

he tried to help get me back where I'd be bound
over to that Farmer Weeks until I was grown up.''

"That's so, Bessie. You wouldn't have much
use for boys if you thought they were all like
him, would you?''

"I know they're not, though, Dolly. So I never
got any such foolish ideas.''

"What sort of things will we do in this field
day, Bessie? Do you know?''

"Not exactly. Miss Mercer hasn't arranged
everything yet with their Scoutmaster, Mr. Hastings. You know the reason we're going to have
it is that Mr. Hastings used to tease Miss Mercer
about the Camp Fire Girls.''

"That's what I thought. He said we really
couldn't manage by ourselves, didn't he, if we
were caught out in the woods without a man to
do a lot of things for us?''

"I think he did. They say a lot of the Boy
Scouts think the Camp Fire Girls are just imitat-
ing them, and that isn't so at all, because I got
Miss Eleanor to tell me all about it. The Camp

Fire Girls are more serious. They want to prepare girls to make good homes, and look after
them properly, and to help them to make things
better in their own homes.

"The Boy Scouts were organized partly to give
boys something to do, and to keep them out in
the open air as much as possible, to make the
boys stronger, and healthier, and keep them from
being idle and getting into mischief."

"Well, that's what we're for, too, isn't it?"

"Yes, but not so much. Girls don't get into
just the same sort of mischief that boys do, so
it's a different thing altogether. But, anyhow,
Miss Eleanor says it's silly for one to laugh and
jeer at the other; that all the Camp Fire people,
the ones who are at the head of the movement,
approve of the Boy Scouts and think it's a fine
thing, and that most of the men who started the
Boy Scout movement are interested in the Camp
Fire, too."

"Then she's going to try to prove that we
really can manage by ourselves?"

"Yes. And I think the idea is for their troop of Boy Scouts and our Camp Fire to make a march on the same day, going about the same distance, and doing everything without any help at all; cooking meals, finding water, making camp, getting firewood, and everything of that sort. A certain time is to be allowed for eating, and we are to make smoke signals when we reach the camping place, and again when we leave. There aren't to be any matches; all fires are to be made by rubbing sticks together. We're to cook just the same sort of meals, and the party that gets back to the starting point first wins."

"We're not to go together, then?"

"No. Won't it be much more exciting? You see, we won't know how nearly finished they are. And they won't be able to see how fast we are working. So each side ought to work just as fast as it can. It's a new sort of a race, and I think it will be great sport."

"Oh, so do I! We're each to spend the same amount of time eating?"

"Yes, because if we didn't, one side could hurry through its meal, or eat almost nothing at all, and get a start that way. And there's no object in eating fast. It's to see how quickly we can march and prepare our food and clean up afterward that we're having the test. It isn't to be exactly like a race. The idea is to get as much fun and good exercise out of it as anything else."

"Still it really will be a race, because each side will want to win. Don't the Boy Scouts have contests like that among themselves, sometimes?"

"Oh, yes. That's where the idea came from, of course."

"My, Bessie, but I'm glad everything is so quiet around here now! It doesn't seem possible that we've had such exciting times since we've been here, does it?"

"You mean about the gypsy who mistook you for me and tried to kidnap you?"

"Yes. I think he's safe for a time now. Did you see Andrew, the guide, when he came in to tell Miss Eleanor about how they'd taken those gypsies down to the town, where the sheriff took hold of them?''

''No. What did he say?''

''Why, it seems that on the way down, John— he's the one who actually carried me off, you know—tried to bribe them and get them to let him go free. He said he had a friend who would pay a whole lot of money if they would let him escape, and they could pretend that he just got away, so that no one would ever know that they had had anything to do with it.''

''I suppose they just laughed at him?''

''They certainly did, and tied him up a little tighter, so that there wouldn't be any chance of his managing to get away.''

''Did he want them to let Lolla and Peter go, too?''

''No, that's the funny part of it. He didn't seem to care at all what happened to them, so long as he didn't have to go to jail. He's just as mean as a snake, Bessie. I've got no use for him at all.''

"He was glad enough to have them help him when he wanted to get hold of us, Dolly. But when he saw a chance to desert them he didn't remember that, I suppose. What did Andrew think they would do to them?"

"Well, he didn't know. He said that when the people in the town heard what the gypsies had done they were pretty mad, but, of course, they didn't really start to do anything to hurt them. The sheriff said he'd see that they were kept tight until they could be tried, and Andrew guessed they wouldn't have much chance of getting off when the people around the town would be on the jury. The men in those parts haven't any use for gypsies, you see, and they'd be pretty sure to see to it that they were properly punished."

"I wouldn't mind seeing Lolla get off, Dolly. I don't think she's as bad as the others."

"Oh, I do, Bessie. I think she's worse. Why, she did her best to get you into the same trap I was in! She was treacherous and lied to you."

"I know all that, too, Dolly. But it was because John made her do it. He frightened her, I think, and besides that she's going to be married to him, and among the gypsies a woman isn't supposed to do any thinking when her husband tells her to do something. She just has to do it, whether she thinks it's right or not. It isn't as if she had planned the whole thing out."

"Well, she hurt you more than she did me. If you don't want her to be punished, I don't see why I should."

"I don't think I want anyone to be punished, Dolly. But it isn't just what I want that counts, and I suppose that if that man John got off so easily it would be a bad thing, because if he's punished it may frighten some others who'd be ready to do the same thing, and make them understand that they'd better be careful before they do things that are against the law."

"Well, I'd like to see him in jail, just to get even for the fright he gave me when he snatched me up and carried me off through the woods.

And he left me there in that place he found, too,
with a handkerchief in my mouth, and tied up
so that I couldn't move, so I don't see why I
shouldn't be glad to see him suffering himself.
It was awful, Bessie, and if you hadn't followed
me and had a chance to sneak in there and cheer
me up, I don't know what I would have done."

"We'll have to tell what we know about what
happened to us, I suppose," said Bessie. "I
don't like the idea of that, but Miss Eleanor
says we can't help it; that the law will make us
do it."

"Oh, I think it will be good fun. We'll get
our names in the newspapers, Bessie, and maybe
there will be pictures of us. I won't have any
trouble telling them, either. I don't believe I'll
ever forget the things that happened to us that
day, if I live to be a hundred years old."

"No, neither shall I."

They had no more chance to discuss the matter,
for just then they heard the voice of Eleanor
Mercer, the Guardian of their Camp Fire, calling

them. When they answered her call, finding her in the opening of her own tent, her face was very grave.

"I've just had a letter from Charlie Jamieson, my cousin, the lawyer," she said. "I wrote to him about the extraordinary attempt that this gypsy made to kidnap Dolly, and of how certain we were that Mr. Holmes was back of it."

"I wish we knew why Mr. Holmes is so anxious to get hold of me, or to get me into the same state I came from, so that Farmer Weeks can keep me there until I'm twenty-one," said Bessie, looking worried.

"I wish so, too, Bessie," said Eleanor, anxiously. "I don't know how much Dolly knows about this business, but I'm very much afraid that she may be drawn into it from now on. And Mr. Jamieson agrees with me."

"Why, how is that possible?" asked Bessie. "You don't mean that they may try to take her away?"

"I don't know, Bessie. That's the worst part

of it. You see, they may think she knows too much for it to be safe to leave her out of any plans they are making now. We don't know what those plans are. This last time, you see, Mr. Holmes evidently thought he had a splendid chance to get hold of you through this gypsy, without being suspected himself.''

''He thought everyone would just blame the gypsy and never think about him at all, you mean?''

''You see, the gypsy misunderstood—or rather Mr. Holmes misled him by accident. He thought Dolly was Bessie, and the other way around. So Dolly really suffered in your place that time, Bessie.''

''I'm very glad I did!'' said Dolly, stoutly.

''I know that, Dolly. You're not selfish, no matter what your other faults may be. But I think you've got to understand just what we know about the reasons for all this, though it isn't very much. Bessie doesn't know much about her parents. They left her—because they had to—when she was a very small girl, in charge of Mr. and Mrs. Hoover, farmers, in Hedgeville."

"I know about that, Miss Eleanor. The place where we first met Bessie and Zara, you mean."

"Yes. And Mrs. Hoover and her son Jake didn't treat Bessie well. In fact, they treated her so badly that finally she ran away. You know that the Camp Fire thinks people ought to stay at home, even if things aren't very pleasant, but Bessie was quite right, I believe, to run away then, because they had no real claim to her."

"I should say she was!"

"Well, you know about Bessie's chum, Zara, too. Her father was in trouble, and was to be arrested. And when Zara and Bessie found out that Zara was to be taken by this Mr. Weeks, a miser and a money lender, Zara ran away, too, and we Camp Fire Girls helped them to get away from that state and have been looking after them since."

"And then they stole Zara away!"

"No, not exactly. They lied to Zara, and told

her things that made her willing to go with them. Mr. Holmes seems to have been responsible for that. You remember yourself how Mr. Holmes tricked you and Bessie into going for a ride with him in his automobile, when we were all at the farm?''

''I certainly do! I ought to, because all the trouble we had then was my own fault.''

''Well, never mind that, because, as it turned out, it was owing to that ride that we got Zara back. She's with us now, and we are going to try to keep her, and get her father out of prison, because Mr. Jamieson is sure he is innocent. But we've got to be mighty careful, because we don't know how Mr. Holmes happens to be mixed up with Farmer Weeks, and why either of them should care anything about Bessie and Zara and Zara's father. That's why I wanted to be sure that you understood as much as we do ourselves.''

''I see, and I'll promise to be as careful as I can, Miss Eleanor. I wouldn't get Bessie or Zara into any more trouble for the world.''

"I know you wouldn't, Dolly, and I hope it won't be very long before the whole thing is straightened out. Mr. Jamieson is working hard to try to find out what it is all about, and I think he's sure to find out soon. This letter I had from him today is a new warning, really. He says Mr. Holmes has hired lawyers to try to get that gypsy off."

"That proves that he hired him, too, I should think," said Bessie.

"It seems to, certainly, but I'm afraid it isn't legal proof, even though it satisfies us. But the chief point is that Mr. Jamieson is worried about you two when you have to testify."

CHAPTER III

"Why, there couldn't be anything they could do to us then, I should think!" exclaimed Dolly.

"I hope not," said Miss Mercer. "But, well, we've had reason to learn to be careful when we're dealing with these people. And Mr. Jamieson seems to think that the thing to fear most is the other gypsies."

"I thought of that, too," said Bessie, gravely. "They stick to one another, don't they?"

"Yes, they certainly do. They're very clannish. And Mr. Holmes, I'm afraid, is clever enough and unscrupulous enough to be willing to use them for his own purposes. He wouldn't tell them directly what he wanted, you see. He'd just hire someone who was clever enough to get them inflamed and worked up to the point of being willing to hurt you two, and, if they could get at her, Zara, too, by way of revenge."

43

"We can't help going down there if they send for us, I suppose, Miss Eleanor?"

"No. There's no way out of it. You see, if someone does you an injury—borrows money from you and doesn't pay it back, say—the law will help you get it, if you want to be helped. You can decide whether you want to do anything or not. But if a crime is committed, then it's a different matter, and you've got to get the law's help, whether you want to or not.

"For instance, if someone robs your house, you might be willing to forgive the robber, but the law has to be satisfied, because that's the sort of crime that affects everyone, and not just you alone."

"I see. And I suppose that this time the law feels that if they are not punished, those gypsies might try to kidnap someone else?"

"Yes. The idea isn't just punishment. It's the way people who live together in towns and countries have to protect themselves. In the early days there wasn't any law. If a man was robbed, and he was strong enough, he protected himself by going out and fighting the robber. But that wouldn't work very well, because if a man was very strong, and wicked as well, he could rob his neighbors, and no one of them was strong enough to protect himself.

"So it wasn't very long before people began to find out that, while no one of them was strong enough to stop such robbers, a whole lot of them banded together were stronger than any one man. And so they made the first laws."

"Oh, I see," said Dolly. "Bessie isn't strong enough by herself to do anything to Mr. Holmes, or to stop him from doing what he likes to her, because he's rich. But if all the other people who live in the state take her side he can't fight against them. That's it, isn't it?"

For a day or two after that peace reigned over the camp by Long Lake. The girls looked forward eagerly to the field day that had been planned, but they looked forward to it, too, with a certain degree of regret, for it would mark the climax and the end, as well, of their stay at the lake, which, though it had been so exciting, had also been so delightful that all the girls wished for nothing better than to stay there indefinitely. But they could not do that, as Miss Mercer explained to them.

"We've got to make way for others," she said, in telling them of the new plans. "You see, my father is only one of the owners of this preserve, and we take it in turns to use this lake for a camping site. Now Mr. Spurgeon, one of the other owners, is going to bring up a party of his friends, and we must make room for them."

"Are we going home?" asked Margery Burton, disappointedly.

"Why, don't you want to go home?" asked Eleanor, with a laugh, which was echoed by the other girls, who heard the note of sorrow in the question.

"Oh, I suppose so," said Margery. "But one is home quite a good deal, after all, in the winter, and we *do* have such a good time when we're out

in the woods this way. I love to get right close
to nature.''

''Well, you needn't be frightened, Margery, because I've got a plan that will keep us as close
to nature as anyone could want to be.''

A chorus of excited voices was raised at that.

''Where are we going next, Miss Mercer?''

''What are we going to do?''

''Shall we get to the seashore this summer?''

''Later on, I expect,'' she answered, to the last
question. ''You do love the beach and the surf,
don't you? Well, so do I, and I expect we shall
want to spend a little time there. But first
I've a plan I think some of you will like even
better.''

''We're sure to like anything you plan, Miss
Eleanor,'' said Dolly, with enthusiasm. ''I don't
believe any Camp Fire has as nice a Guardian
as you. It seems to me you spend all your time
thinking up ways of giving us a good time.''

''What is the new plan?'' asked Margery. ''I
wonder if I can guess?''

"I don't know. You might all try, and see how near you come to it."

"I think we're going to go home by walking!" said Margery.

"I believe we'll go through the chain of lakes that begins at Little Bear in a boat, or in boats!" said Dolly.

But, though they all took turns in guessing, Eleanor only smiled wisely when the last guess had been made.

"You were very nearly right, Margery," she said. "We are going to tramp home, but not the way we came. We're going to take the long way round. We're going straight up and through the mountains and down the other side, and then we'll have a long trip on fairly level ground, but we won't go straight home."

"Where, then?" asked Dolly.

"Why, we'll combine everything on the one trip, Dolly, and we'll wind up at the seashore. By the time we've had a little swimming and sailing there it'll be time to think about what we're going to do in the autumn—school, and work, and all the other things."

"Oh, that's splendid!" cried Margery, her eyes shining. "I've always wanted to go up in the real mountains, where you were so high that you could see all around the country. We'll do that, won't we? Here we're in the mountains, really, but it doesn't seem like it. Everything's so high, you can't see over."

Eleanor pointed to the distant hills, blue in the haze that hung over them.

"Do you see Mount Grant, the big one in the center, there?" she said. "And do you see that other mountain that seems to be right next to it? That's Mount Sherman. And right between them there's a little gap. Really, it's quite wide, though you can't tell that from here. Well, that's Indian Notch, and we get through the mountain range by going through it. It's a fine, wild country, but there's a good road through the notch now, and sometimes one meets quite a lot of automobiles going through. I think it will be a glorious trip, don't you, girls?"

"I certainly do!" said Bessie King. "I'm like Margery. I've always wanted to see the real mountains. I used to dream about them, and sometimes I'd think I'd really been there. But I guess it was just because I dreamed so much that I got to thinking so."

Eleanor looked at her curiously.

"Maybe your people came from the mountains, Bessie," she said. "It's very strange that some natural things seem to get into the blood of peoples and races. Like the mountains, and the sea, and great rivers. Sometimes all the men in a family, for generations, will be sailors, even if their parents have planned something else for them. The sea is in their blood, and it calls them."

"Sometimes I think the mountains are calling me just that way," said Bessie. "But I never really understood that before."

"It's the same way with mountaineers. The

Swiss are never really happy except among their mountains. And that's true of every mountainous race. The people who live along the Mississippi, here, and along the Don and the Vistula, and the other great rivers in Russia, never seem to be able to live happily unless they can see the great river rolling by their homes every day. If they go far away they get homesick.''

"I'm not a bit like that!" exclaimed Dolly. "One place is just as good as another for me, if I like the people. I like to travel and see new places. I'd like to be on the move all the time.''

"I think a great many Americans are getting to be that way," said Eleanor, reflectively. "It's natural, in a way, you see. For generations the young men and women have been moving on, from settled parts of the country to new land, where there were greater opportunities to make a fortune.''

"I've read about that," said Dolly. "You mean like the people from New England, who went west to Oregon and Washington?''

"Yes. But that can't go on forever, you see, because about all the new land is taken up and settled now. Of course, out in the far west, there's still room for people; lots and lots of room. But this whole country is settled now. Law and order have been established about everywhere. And we'll begin to settle down soon, and our people will love their homes, and the places where they were born, just as the Virginians and the other Southerners do now."

"Oh, it isn't that I don't like my own home!" said Dolly. "If I were away from it very long I know I'd get dreadfully homesick, and want to go back. But I don't want to stay there or anywhere else all the time."

"You're a wanderer," laughed Eleanor. "That's what's the matter with you, Dolly. You want to see everything that's to be seen. Well, I'm a little that way myself. When I was a little bit of a kiddie I always got tremendously excited if we were going on a journey. I guess it's a pretty good thing, really, that we are that way.

It's the reason this country has grown so wonderfully, that spirit of enterprise and adventure. That's what made the pioneers."

"It isn't just Americans who do it, either, is it?" said Margery. "The Italians and the other foreigners who come here seem to be just as anxious to find new places—"

"Oh, but that's different," said Zara, the silent one, quickly. "I know, because my father and I are foreigners. And do you know why we came here? It was because we couldn't live happily in our own country!"

The girls looked at her curiously, so fiery was her speech, and so much in earnest was she.

"We come from Poland," she said. "Over there, a man can't call his soul his own. Soldiers and policemen used to come to our house, and wake us up in the middle of the night to look for papers. And often and often they would steal anything we had that they liked. Oh, how I hate the Russians!"

Eleanor sighed. Gradually, slowly but surely,

she felt that she was finding her way into the secret of Zara and her father.

"Then you came here because you had heard that this was a free country and a refuge for those who were oppressed?" she ventured, gently.

"Yes," said Zara. "And it's not true! There are kind people here, like you, and Bessie, and Mr. Jamieson. But haven't they put my father in prison, just the way they did in Poland and in Sicily, when we tried to live there quietly? And didn't all the people in Hedgeville persecute him, and tell lies about both of us? We haven't been happy here."

"I'm afraid that's true, Zara. But you are going to be, remember that. You have good friends working for you now, you and your father both. And it isn't the fault of this country that there are bad and wicked men in it, who are willing to do wrong if they see a chance to make money by doing so."

"But if this country is all that people say about it, they shouldn't be allowed to do it. The law is helping them. In Poland, it was just the same. The law was against my father there—''

"Listen, Zara! The law may seem to help them at first, but you may be very sure of one thing. If your father has done nothing wrong, and his enemies have lied and deceived the people in authority in order to get the law on their side, they will pay bitterly for it in the end.''

"But the law ought to know that my father is right—''

"The law works slowly, Zara, but in the end it is sure to be right. You see, your father's case is a very exceptional one. The people who made the law in the beginning couldn't have expected it to come. But the wonderful thing about the law is that, while it is often very hard, it will always find out the truth sooner or later.

"Sometimes, for a little while, people who are innocent have to suffer because they are unjustly accused. But the law will free them if they have really done no wrong, and, what is more, it will punish those who swear falsely against them. Be patient, and you will find that you and your father made no mistake when you believed that this was the land of the free and the home of those who are oppressed in their own countries.''

Zara's eyes, dark and sombre, seemed to be full of fire.

''Oh, I hope so,'' she cried, passionately. ''For my father's sake! He has been disappointed and deceived so often.''

''We'll have a good long talk sometime, Zara,'' she said, finally. ''Then maybe I'll be able to explain some things to you better, and make you understand the real difference between this country and the ones you have known.''

Then she brightened, and turned to the other girls, who had all been rather sobered by the sudden revelation, through Zara, of a side of life hidden from them as a rule.

''We're not going to take that trip just for ourselves and our own fun,'' she said. ''We're going to be missionaries, in a way; we want to spread the light of the Camp Fire, and see if we

can't get a lot of new Camp Fires organized in
the places we pass through. It's just in such
lonely, country places that the girls need the Camp
Fire most, I believe.''

"That will be splendid," said Margery Burton.
"We could stay and teach them all the ceremonies,
and the songs, and how to organize new Camp
Fires, couldn't we?"

"Yes. We want to make them see how much
it has done for us. When they know that they'll
do the rest for themselves, I think. I shall expect
all you girls to help, because you can do ever so
much more than I. It's the girls who really count
—not the Guardians, you know."

CHAPTER IV

A FRIEND IN TROUBLE

The next morning Eleanor Mercer, summoned from the group of girls with whom she was discussing some details of the coming contest with the Boy Scouts by the appearance of a man who had rowed up to the little landing stage, accompanied by one of the guides, old Andrew, called Bessie King and Dolly Ransom to her with a grave face.

"This is Deputy Sheriff Rogers, from Hamilton," she explained. "He says that you must go there today to testify against those gypsies."

"Sorry, ma'am, if it's awkward jest now," said the officer. "But law's law, and orders is orders."

"Oh, we understand that perfectly, Mr. Rogers," said Eleanor. "You have to do your duty, and of course we are anxious to see that the law

59

is properly enforced. Don't think we're complaining. But I will admit I am nervous."

"Nervous, ma'am? Why, there ain't nothin' to be nervous about!"

"I hope you're right, Mr. Rogers. But there are things back of this attempt to kidnap my two girls here that haven't come out at all yet. I don't suppose you've heard of them. And it's been suggested to me that it might not be quite safe for them at Hamilton."

The deputy sheriff laughed heartily at that.

"Safe?" he said. "Well, I should some guess they'll be safe down there! Sheriff Blaine—he's my boss, ma'am, you see—would jest about rip the hide off of anyone who tried to tech them young ladies while they was there obeyin' the orders of the court. Don't you worry none. We'll look after them all right enough."

"As long as you know that there may be some danger, I shall be relieved, and feel that everything is all right," said Eleanor, pleasantly. "It's when we're not expecting their blows that the

people we are afraid of have been able to strike
at us successfully. There is a Mr. Holmes—''

''I know him well, if it's Mr. Holmes, the big
storekeeper from the city you mean, ma'am,'' interrupted Rogers. ''Say, if he's a friend of yours,
you can be sure you'll be looked after all right
down to Hamilton. We think a sight of him down
there. He's a fine man, ma'am; yes, indeed, a fine
man!''

Eleanor looked startled, and only Bessie's quick
pinch of her arm prevented Dolly from crying out
in surprise and disgust. Knowing what they did
of the treachery and meanness of Holmes, this
praise of him was disturbing to a degree. But
Eleanor never changed countenance. She understood, as if by some instinct, that this was a time
for keeping her own counsel.

''I shall go to Hamilton with you,'' said Eleanor,
decidedly. ''Will you be able to wait a little while,
Mr. Rogers, while we get ready?''

''Surely, ma'am,'' said Rogers. ''We want to
get the train that goes down from the station here

at noon, and that gives us lots of time. If we start two hours from now we'll catch it, with time to spare.''

''Then if you'll sit down and make yourself comfortable,'' she said, ''we'll be ready when it's time to start.''

As soon as Rogers had taken himself off, Eleanor called the girls together in her own tent.

''I feel that it is my duty to be with Bessie and Dolly at Hamilton,'' she explained. ''And, because I rather foresaw this, I have arranged for a friend of mine to come over here and take my place as Guardian at short notice. She is Miss Drew—Miss Anna Drew—and some of you must have met her in the city. She has had plenty of experience as a Camp Fire Guardian, and you'll all like her, I know.

''Please make it as easy for her as possible. Do just as she tells you, even if she doesn't have the same way of doing everything that I have. I'll get back as soon as I can, and I want you to have a good time while we're gone.''

"We'll see that she doesn't have any trouble, Wanaka," said Margery Burton loyally. "She'll find that this Camp Fire can behave itself, all right!"

"Thanks! I knew I could count on all of you," said Eleanor. "Now I'm going to send her a note by Andrew. Her people own some of this land, and she happens to be in their camp at one of the other lakes, so that she'll be able to get here before we go if she starts at once."

Andrew was quite ready to carry the note, and went off while Eleanor and the two girls made the simple preparations that were necessary for their trip.

"I'm so glad you didn't say anything when the deputy sheriff spoke that way of Mr. Holmes," she said to Bessie and Dolly. "I was afraid one of you would cry out and I really couldn't have blamed you if you had."

"I would have—I was just going to," said Dolly honestly, "but Bessie pinched me, so I shut up, though I couldn't see why. I still think he ought to know that this man he seems to think so much of is the very one they ought to watch most carefully if they really want to make sure that we don't get into any trouble while we're going down there.''

"The trouble is that he wouldn't believe it, Dolly, and it would simply discredit us with him and all the other authorities at Hamilton, so that they wouldn't believe us when we had something to tell them that we were sure was true.''

"But we're sure that Mr. Holmes was behind this gypsy. We've got the letter he wrote to him to prove it!''

"Yes, but Mr. Jamieson doesn't want anyone to know we have that letter until the proper time comes. He wants to catch Mr. Holmes in a trap if he possibly can, so that he'll be harmless after this. You ´can see what a good thing that would be.''

"Oh, yes. I never thought of that! He doesn't want to put him on his guard, you mean?''

"Just exactly that, Dolly. You see, if Mr. Holmes thinks we don't suspect him, it's possible that he may betray himself in some fashion. He'll feel sure that this man John hasn't betrayed him, and if he thinks we don't know anything about the part he had in this kidnapping plan, he may try to do something else that will get him into serious trouble.

"And we've got to move very slowly and very carefully, because it's quite plain that he has a lot of friends at Hamilton and that they won't believe anything against him, no matter how serious it may be, unless they get absolute proof."

"Oh, I do hope Mr. Jamieson will be able to catch him this time! I'd feel ever so much better about Bessie and Zara if I knew that they didn't need to be afraid of him any longer."

"So would I, Dolly, and so would Mr. Jamieson. It's this man who is worrying us more than all the other enemies Bessie and Zara have, put together."

5

"Because he's so rich?"

"Partly that, and because he's so clever, too. And if all I hear about him is true, the more he is beaten, the more dangerous he becomes. He doesn't like to be beaten, and it makes him so angry that he takes all sorts of chances, and does the wildest, most desperate things to get even. They say he was very unfair to a lot of small shopkeepers in the city when he was building up his big store."

"How do you mean, Miss Eleanor?"

"Why, he did everything he could to make them sell out to him for a small price, and, if they wouldn't do it, he did his best to ruin their business. He would circulate false stories about them, and he used his influence with the police and the city authorities to make all sorts of trouble for them.

"Then he would open a store next door to them, sometimes, and sell everything they did cheaper, at a loss, so that people would stop buying from them. You see, he could afford to lose money doing

that, because he knew that if he once got them out
of the way, he could put prices up again, and get
his money back.''

"You didn't know all that the day after Zara
was taken away, did you, Miss Eleanor?" asked
Bessie. "Don't you remember how you laughed
at me then for saying I didn't like him, and that I
thought he might be mixed up in Zara's disap-
pearance?"

"Yes, I do remember it very well, Bessie. I've
often thought what a good thing it was that your
eyes were so sharp, and that you suspected him
even when all the rest of us thought he was all
right. If it hadn't been for that, Mr. Jamieson
would never have looked up the records that gave
him the clue to where Mr. Holmes had hidden
Zara.''

"I think Bessie would make a pretty good detective," said Dolly. "They do have women de-
tectives now, don't they? And she seems to be
able to tell from looking at people whether they
can be trusted or not.''

Bessie laughed heartily at that suggestion.

"I can't do anything of the sort," she said. "And, even if I could, I wouldn't be a detective, Dolly. The trouble with you is that you read too many novels. You think people behave in real life just the way the people in the books you read do, and they don't."

The return of old Andrew, the guide, who had rowed across the lake on his return from carrying Eleanor's note to Miss Drew, was the signal to complete the preparations for departure.

"I caught her, all right, Miss Eleanor," said Andrew. "Says she won't be able to come over here till after lunch, but she'll be right over then with a bundle of sticks to keep the young ladies in order till you get back yourself."

"Good!" laughed Eleanor. "That's all right, then, and I can leave here with a clear conscience. Andrew, you'll sort of keep an eye on things till I get back, won't you?"

"Leave it to me, ma'am," said Andrew. "Say, me and some of the boys was thinking maybe you'd like to have some of us turn up, sort of casual like, down at Hamilton?''

''Why, it's very good of you, Andrew, but I don't believe we'll need any help from you, thanks.''

''You can't always sometimes tell,'' said Andrew, sagely. ''Now, this here Rogers is a good fellow enough, but obstinate as a mule, and the sheriff might be his twin brother for that. They're birds of a feather, see? And onct they get it into their heads that a thing's so, there ain't nothin' I know of, short of a stick of dynamite, will make them change their minds. So we thought that mebbe it wouldn't be a bad idea to have some of us within call.''

''I'll let you know if we need any help, Andrew,'' promised Eleanor. ''And it's very good of you to offer to come. But Mr. Jamieson will be there—you know him, don't you?''

''Mister Charlie? Indeed I do, ma'am, and a fine young chap he is, too. I've often hunted with him through these woods up here. If he's goin'

to look after the law part of this for you, you'll
have a good chance to beat them sharks down
there. Some pretty smart lawyers there at Hamilton, they tell me, ma'am. I ain't never been to
law myself. Any time I get into a fight I can't
settle with my tongue, I use my hands. Cheaper,
and better, too, in the long run.''

''It's the old-fashioned way, Andrew. Most
people can't settle their troubles so easily. Well,
you'll row us to the end of the lake, I suppose?''

''Get right in, ma'am! Might as well start, so's
you can take it easy on the trail. Not a bit of
use hurryin' when there ain't no need of it, I
say. There's lots of times when it can't be helped,
without lookin' for a chance.''

So, with the strains of the Wo-he-lo cheer rising
from the girls who were left behind, they started
in the boat for the first stage of the short journey
to Hamilton.

Andrew insisted on going with them as far as
the station, and as the train pulled out, they heard
his cheery voice.

"Now, remember if you need me or any of the boys, all you've got to do is to send us word, and we'll find a way to get there a bit quicker than we're expected," he cried. "Ain't nothin' we wouldn't do for you and the young ladies, Miss Eleanor!"

"You leave them to us, old timer," Rogers called back from the car window. "We'll guarantee to return them, safe and sound. And it won't take any long time, neither. There's a good case against that sneaking gypsy, and we'll have him on his way to the penitentiary in two shakes of a lamb's tail."

"If you don't, I'll vote for another sheriff next election," vowed Andrew, "if I have to vote a Demmycratic ticket to do it, and that's somethin' I ain't done—not since I was old enough to vote."

Rogers was reassuring enough in his speech and manner, but Eleanor had a presentiment of evil; a foreboding that something was wrong.

The railroad trip to Hamilton was not a long one, and within two hours of the time they had left Long Lake the brakeman called out the name of the county seat. Eleanor and the two girls, with Rogers carrying their bags, moved to the door, and, as they reached the ground, looked about eagerly for Jamieson.

He was nowhere to be seen. But Holmes was there, avoiding their eyes, but with a grin of malicious triumph that worried Eleanor. And Rogers, a moment after he had left them to speak to a friend, returned, his face grave.

"I hear your friend Mr. Jamieson is arrested," he said.

CHAPTER V

"Arrested?" cried Eleanor, startled. "Why, what do you mean? How can that be?"

"That's all I know, ma'am," said Rogers, soberly. "Even if I did know anything more, I guess maybe I oughtn't to be saying anything about it. I'm an officer, you see. But here's the district attorney. Maybe he'll be able to tell you what you want."

He pointed to a tall, thin man who was talking earnestly to Holmes, and who came over when Rogers beckoned to him.

"This is Mr. Niles, Miss Mercer," said Rogers. "I'll leave you with him."

"Glad to meet you, Miss Mercer," said Niles, heartily, "though I'm sorry to have dragged you away from your good times at Long Lake. These, I suppose, are the young ladies who were kidnapped?"

73

"Yes, though of course they weren't really kidnapped, because they got away before any real harm was done," Eleanor replied. "But, Mr. Niles, what is this absurd story about my cousin, Mr. Jamieson? Mr. Rogers said something about his having been arrested."

Niles grew grave.

"I hope you're right—I hope it is absurd, my dear young lady," he said. "Your cousin, you say? Dear me, that's most distressing—most distressing, upon my word! However, you will understand I had nothing to do with the matter.

"I have to take cognizance, in my official capacity, of any charges that are made, but I am allowed to have my own opinion as to the guilt or innocence of those accused—yes, indeed! And I am quite sure that Mr. Jamieson had nothing to do with this attempted kidnapping!"

"What?" gasped Eleanor. "Do you mean to say that it is on such a charge as that that he has been arrested?"

She laughed, in sheer relief. The absurdity of

such an accusation, she was sure, would carry
proof in itself that Charlie was innocent. No matter who was trying to spoil his reputation, they
could not possibly succeed with such a flimsy and
silly charge.

"I'm glad it seems so funny to you, Miss Mercer," said Niles, stiffly. "I'll confess that it looked
serious to me, although, as I say, I do not believe
in Mr. Jamieson's guilt. However, he will have
to clear himself, of course, just as anyone else
accused of a crime must do. Where I have juris-
diction, no favors are shown.

"The poor are on a basis of equality with the
rich; I would send a guilty millionaire to prison
with a light heart, and on the same day I would
move heaven and earth to secure the freedom of
an innocent beggar, though men of wealth were
trying to railroad him to jail!"

He finished that peroration with a sweeping and
dignified bow. And then he stopped, thunder-
struck, as a clear, girlish laugh rose on the air.
It was Dolly who laughed.

"I couldn't help it," she said, afterward. "He was so funny, and he didn't know it! As if anyone would take a man who talked such rot as that seriously!"

But the trouble was that, vain and pompous as Niles plainly was, his official position made it necessary to take him seriously. Though at first she was disposed to agree with Dolly, and had, indeed, had difficulty in keeping a straight face herself while he was boasting of his own incorruptibility, Eleanor discovered that fact as soon as she had a chance to talk with Charlie Jamieson.

"I shall be glad to arrange for you to have an interview with your cousin, Miss Mercer," Niles informed her. "Theoretically, he is a prisoner, although of course he will be able to arrange for his own release on bail as soon as he finds some friend who owns property in this county. But I have given orders that he is not to be confined in a cell. I trust he is making himself very much at home in the parlor of Sheriff Blaine. If you will honor me, I will take you there."

"I should like to see him at once," said Eleanor. "Come, girls! Mr. Niles, I am sure, will find a place where you can wait for me while I talk with Mr. Jamieson."

Charlie greeted her with a sour grin when she was taken to the room where, a prisoner, he was sitting near a window and smoking some of the sheriff's excellent tobacco.

"Hello, Nell!" he said. "First blood for our friend Holmes on this scrap, all right. First time I've ever been in jail. It's intended as a little object lesson of what he can do when he once starts out to be unpleasant, I fancy. He must know that he hasn't any sort of chance of keeping me here."

"Why, Charlie, I never heard anything so absurd!" said Eleanor, hotly. "As if you, who have done everything possible for those girls, would do such an insane thing as hire that gypsy to kidnap them. And especially when we know who did do it!"

"That's just the rub! We know, but can we

prove it? You see, it's my idea that Holmes is
starting this as a sort of backfire. He thinks we're
going to accuse him, and he wants to strike the
first blow. He's clever, all right."

"I don't see what good it can do him, Charlie."

"A lot of good, and this is why. He puts me on
the defensive, right away. He wants time as much
as anything else. And if he can keep me busy prov-
ing my own innocence, he figures that I'll have
less time to get after him. It's a good move. The
more chance he has to work on those gypsies,
the less likely they are to say anything that
will make trouble for him. He can show them
his power and scare them, even if he can't buy
them.

"And I think the chances are that he won't
find it very hard to buy them. They pinched me
as soon as I got off the train this morning. I've
sent out a lot of telegrams, asking fellows to come
up here and bail me out, but of course I can't
really expect to get an answer today—an answer in
person, at least."

"Mr. Niles seems friendly. He said that he doesn't believe you're guilty, Charlie."

"That's kind of him, I'm sure. Niles is an ass—a pompous, self-satisfied ass! Holmes is using him just as he likes, and Niles hasn't got sense enough to see it. He's honest enough, I think, but he hasn't got the brains of a well-developed jellyfish."

Eleanor laughed at the comparison.

"Well, if he's honest, you don't have anything to fear, I suppose," she said. "I'm glad of that, Charlie. I was afraid at first that he might be just a tool of Mr. Holmes, and that he would do what Mr. Holmes told him."

"I'd feel easier in my mind if he were a regular out-and-out crook, Nell. That sort always has a weakness. Your crook is afraid of his own skin, and when he knows he's doing things for pay, he'll always stop just short of a certain danger point. He won't risk more than so much for anyone. But with this chap it's different. He's probably let Holmes, or Holmes's gang, fill him up

with a lot of false ideas, and they're clever enough
to get him to wanting to do just what they want
him to do.''

''And you mean that he'll think he's doing the
right thing?''

''Yes, and not only that, but he'll persuade himself that he figured the whole thing out, thought
it out for himself, when really he'll just be carrying out their own suggestions. We've got to
find some way to spike his guns, or else Holmes
will work things so that his gypsy will get off, and
there'll be no sort of chance to pin the guilt down
to him, where it belongs.''

''Then the first thing to do is to get you out,
isn't it?''

''Yes, but I've done all that can be done on
that. There's really nothing to be done now but
just wait—and I'd rather do pretty nearly anything I can think of but that.''

''I don't know, Charlie. Why can't I give bail
for you? You know, Dad made over all that land
up in the woods around Long Lake that he owns to

me. So I'm a property holder in this county—
and that's what is needed, isn't it?"

"By Jove! You're right, Nell! Here, I'll make
out an application. You send for Niles, and we'll
get him to approve this right now. Then we'll get
the judge to sign the bail bond, and I'll get out. ·
I never thought of that—good thing you've got a
good head on your shoulders!"

Eleanor, pleased and excited, went out to find
Niles, and returned to Charlie with him at once.

"H'm, bail has been fixed at a nominal figure—
five thousand dollars," said Niles. "I may men-
tion that I suggested it, knowing that you would
not try to evade the issue, Mr. Jamieson. We have
heard of you, sir, even up here. If the young lady
will come to the judge's office with me, I have no
doubt we can arrange the matter."

Before long it was evident there was a hitch.

"I am sorry, Miss Mercer," said Niles, with a
long face, "but there seems to be some doubt as to
this. You have not the deed with you—the deed
giving title to this property?"

4—C6

"No," said Eleanor. "But the records are here, are they not? Certainly you can make sure that I own it?"

Niles shook his head.

"I'm afraid we must have the deed," he said.

For the moment it looked as if Charlie would have to stay in confinement over night, at least. But suddenly Eleanor remembered old Andrew and his offer to help. And twenty minutes later she was explaining matters to him over the telephone.

"Why, sure," he said. "I can fix you up, Miss Eleanor. I've saved money since I've been working here, and I've put it all into land. I know these woods, you see, and I know that when I get ready to sell I'll get my profit. I'll be down as soon as I can come."

"Don't say a word," said Charlie. "It wouldn't be past them to fake some way of clouding the old man's title if they knew he was coming. We'll spring that on them as a surprise. Evidently

they figure on being able to keep me here until
to-morrow, at least. They've got some scheme on
foot—they've got a card up their sleeves that
they want to be able to play while I'm not watching
them. I don't just get on to their game—it's hard
to figure it out from here. But if I once get out I
won't be afraid of them. We'll be able to beat
them, all right, thanks to you. You're a brick,
Nell!''

Andrew was as good as his word. He reached
the town in time to go to the judge with the deeds
of his property, and though Holmes, who was
evidently watching every move of the other side
closely, scowled and looked as if he would like
to make some protest, there was nothing to be
done. He and his lawyers had no official standing in the case—they could only consult with and
advise Niles in an unofficial fashion. And,
though Niles held a long conference with Holmes
and his party before the bail bond was signed, it
proved to be impossible for the court to decline
to accept it. Some things the law made impera-

tive, and, much as Niles might feel that he was being tricked, he could not help himself.

Once he was free, as he was when the bail bond was signed, Jamieson wasted no time. He saw Eleanor and the two girls settled in the one good hotel of Hamilton, and then rushed back to the court house. And there he found a strange state of affairs. Holmes had brought with him from the city two lawyers, though Isaac Brack, the shyster, was not one of them. And the leader, a man well known to Jamieson, John Curtin by name, now appeared boldly as the lawyer for the accused gypsies. Moreover, he refused absolutely to allow Charlie to see his clients.

In answer to Charlie's protests he merely looked wise, and refused to say anything more than was required to reiterate his refusal. But Charlie had other sources of information, and an hour after his release, meeting Eleanor, who had walked down to look around the town, leaving the girls behind at the hotel, he gave her some startling news.

"They're trying to get those gypsies out right now," he said. "They were indicted, you know, for kidnapping. Now Curtis has got a writ of habeas corpus, and he's kept it so quiet that it was only by accident I found it was to be argued."

"What does that mean?" asked Eleanor. "I don't know as much about the law as you do, you know."

"It means that a judge will decide whether they are being legally held or not, Nell. And it looks very much to me as if Holmes had managed to fix things so that they'll get off without ever going before a jury at all! Niles isn't handling the case right. He's allowed Holmes and his crowd to pull the wool over his eyes completely. If we had some definite proof I could force him to hold them. But—"

Eleanor laughed suddenly.

"I didn't suppose it was necessary to give this to you until the trial," she said. "But look here, Charlie—isn't this proof?" And she handed him the letter found on John, the gypsy—a letter from

Holmes, giving him the orders that led to the kidnapping of Dolly.

Charlie shouted excitedly when he read it.

"By Jove!" he said. "This puts them in our power. You were quite right—we don't want to produce this yet. But I think I can use it to scare our friend Niles. If I'm right, and he's only a fool, and not a knave, I'll be able to do the trick. Here he is now! Watch me give him the shock of his young life!"

Niles approached, with a sweeping bow for Eleanor, and a cold nod for Jamieson. But the city lawyer approached him at once.

"How about this habeas corpus hearing, Mr. District Attorney?" he asked. "Are you going to let them get those gypsies out of jail?"

"The case against them appears to be hopelessly defective, sir," returned Niles, stiffly. "I am informed by counsel for the defense that there are a number of witnesses to prove an alibi for the man John, and, I feel that it is useless to try to have them held for trial."

"Suppose I tell you that I have absolute evidence—evidence connecting them with the plot, and bringing in another conspirator who has not yet been named? Hold on, Mr. Niles, you have been tricked in this case. I don't hold it against you, but I warn you that if you don't make a fight in this case, papers charging you with incompetence will go to the governor at once, with a petition for your removal!"

"I—I don't know why I should allow one of the prisoners in this case to address me in such a fashion!" stuttered Niles.

"I don't care what you know! I'm telling you the truth, and, for your own sake, you'd better listen to me," said Jamieson, grimly. "I mean just what I say. And unless you want to be lined up with your friend Curtin in disbarment proceedings, you'd better cut loose from him. I suppose Holmes has told you he'll back your ambitions to go to Congress, hasn't he?"

Niles seemed to be staggered.

"How—how did you know that?" he gasped.

As a matter of fact, Charlie had not known it;
he had only made a shrewd guess. But the shot
had gone home.

"There's more to this than you can guess, Mr.
Niles," he said, more kindly. "It's a plot that is
bigger than even I can understand and they have
simply tried to use you as a tool. I knew that once
you had a hint of the truth, your native shrewd-
ness would make you work to defeat it. You understand, don't you?"

Coming on top of the bullying, this sop to the
love of Niles for flattery was thoroughly effective.
Charlie was using the same sort of weapons that
the other side had employed. And Niles held out
his hand.

"I'll take the chance," he said. "I'll see that
those fellows stay in jail, Mr. Jamieson. As I
told Miss Mercer, I was sure from the beginning
that you were all right. May I count on you for
aid when the case comes up for trial?"

"You may—and I'll give you a bigger prisoner
than you ever thought of catching," said Charlie.

CHAPTER VI

BESSIE KING'S PLUCK

"We've got them, I think," Jamieson said to Eleanor Mercer and the two girls after his talk with District Attorney Niles. "There's just one thing; I don't understand how Holmes can be so reckless as to take a chance when he must remember that he hasn't got a leg left to stand on."

"He probably doesn't know that we know anything about it," said Bessie. "And I guess he thinks that if we had had that note all this time we'd have produced it before, so that he thought it was safe to act."

"You're probably right, Bessie," said Eleanor. "I thought that letter would be useful, Charlie, when we took it from that gypsy. I don't suppose I really had any right to keep it, but just then, you see, Andrew and the other guides were

89

the only people around, and they would never question anything I did—they'd just be sure I was right."

"Good thing they do, for you usually are," laughed Charlie. "I've given up expecting to catch you, Nell. You guess right too often. And this time you've certainly called the turn. Niles is convinced. All I'm afraid of now is that he won't be able to hold his tongue."

"You want to surprise Mr. Holmes, then?"

"I certainly do. I'd give a hundred dollars right now to see his face when I spring that letter and ask for a warrant for his arrest. Mind you, I don't suppose for a minute we'll be able to do him any real harm. He's got too much influence, altogether, with bigger people than Niles and this judge here."

"You know I'm not very vindictive, Charlie, but I would like to see him get the punishment he deserves. I'd much rather have them let those poor gypsies off, if only they would put him in prison in their place. I feel sorry for them—

really, I do. It seems to me that they were just led astray by a man who certainly should know better.''

''That part of it's all right enough, Eleanor. But if one accepted the excuse from every criminal that he was led astray by a stronger character, no one would ever be punished. Pretty nearly everyone who ever gets arrested can frame up that excuse.''

''You don't think it's a good one?''

''It is, to a certain extent. But if our way of punishing people for doing wrong is any good at all, and if it is really to have any good effect, it's got to teach the weaklings that every man is responsible himself for what he does, that he can't shift the blame to someone else and get out of it that way.

''You remember the poem Kipling wrote about that? I mean that line that goes: 'The sins that we sin by two and two we must pay for one by one.' It seems pretty hard sometimes, but it's got to be done. However, even if Holmes gets out of

this, it's a thundering good thing that we've got
as much as we have against him.''

"I don't see why, if you say he's going to get
off without punishment.''

"Well, I think it's apt to make him more careful, for one thing. And for another, some people
will believe the evidence against him, and he'll
have the punishment of being partly discredited
at least. That's better than nothing, you know.
One reason he's in a position to do these rotten
things without fear of being caught is that he's
supposed to be so respectable. Let people once
begin to think he isn't any better than he should
be, and he'll have to mind his p's and q's just
like anyone else, I can tell you.''

"That's so! I didn't think of that.''

"The thing to do now is to make sure that the
trial comes off at once. I've got an idea that
they'll try to get a delay, now that they've had to
give up their hope of rushing it through while I
was tied up and couldn't tell whatever I happened
to know. They'll figure that the more time they

have, the more chance there is that they can work out some new scheme, or that something will turn up in their favor—some piece of luck. And it's just as likely to happen as not to happen, too, if we give them a chance to hold things up for a few weeks. You want to get away, too, don't you?"

"We certainly do, Charlie. The girls would be dreadfully disappointed if we didn't get back in time to make the tramp through the mountains with them."

"Well, I guess we'll manage it all right. Leave that to me. You've had bothers and troubles enough already since you got here. I ought to have a nurse! Here I come to look after your interests, and see that nothing goes wrong with you and your affairs, and the first thing you have to do is to get me out of jail!"

Eleanor returned his laugh.

"We really enjoyed it, though you've got Andrew to thank, not me," she said. "Do you really think they'll manage to get it postponed after tomorrow?"

"Not if I have to sit up with Niles and hold his hand all night, to keep him in line," vowed Jamieson.

And, indeed, the morning proved that there was no cause for worry. Niles, stiffened by Jamieson, refused even to see the men from the other side, who were employed by Holmes, when they came to his office to beg for an adjournment, or to ask him to consent to it, at least, since only the judge had the power to grant it. And the trial began at the appointed time.

Charlie, not being actively engaged as a lawyer in the case, could not spring his sensation himself. But he sat near Niles, waiting for the opportune moment, and, before the morning session was over, since he saw that the time was drawing near, he wrote a note to Niles, explaining his plan to surprise Holmes fully, which he handed to him in the quiet courtroom.

"That's great—great!" said Niles. "It's immense, Jamieson! I never dreamed of anything like that. Heavens! How I have been deceived in this man Holmes! You have the original letter, you say?"

Jamieson tapped his breast pocket significantly.

"You bet I've got it!" he said. "And it doesn't leave my possession, either, until it's been read into the records of this court. You'll have to call me as a witness, Niles. That's the only way we can get this over, since I can't very well act as counsel for either side of the case."

"All right. First thing after lunch," said Niles.

Holmes was in the courtroom, and Jamieson, happening to look up just as Niles spoke to him, caught the merchant pointing to him, the while he bent over and talked earnestly with a sinister, scowling man who was unknown to the lawyer, but who seemed to be on the most intimate terms with Holmes. However, he thought nothing of the incident. He had understood from the first that in opposing Holmes, and doing all he could to spoil his plans regarding Bessie and Zara, he was incurring the millionaire's enmity, and he did not greatly care.

"You know," he had said to Eleanor, "this chap
Holmes thinks—or he did think, at least—that I'd
be scared by his ability to help or hurt a man in
my profession in the city. But I think a whole lot
of that is bluff on his part. I don't believe he can
do as much as he thinks he can. And I don't know
that I care a whole lot, anyhow. He hasn't gone
out of his way to help me so far, and I've managed
to get along pretty well. I guess I can do without
him to the end of the chapter."

Just after the court adjourned for lunch, Niles
was called away by Curtin, the leader of the lawyers Holmes had hired to defend the gypsy prisoners, and Jamieson saw them talking earnestly together for several minutes. Naturally, he did not
try to overhear the conversation, but he could not
have done so in any case, for Curtin kept looking
about him, so that it was evident that he, at least,
regarded what he had to say as both important and
confidential. But Charlie waited patiently, sure
that Niles would tell him all he wanted to know,
unless he should again go over to the other side.

"They're wise to us," said Niles, when he returned. "Curtin knows we've got something up our sleeves, and maybe he wasn't anxious to find out what it was!"

"You didn't tell him, I hope?"

"Not I! Trust me to know better than that! But I think he's got an inkling."

"Lord, why shouldn't he?" said Charlie to himself, bitterly. "Of course, there's no reason why that gypsy shouldn't tell him! He probably doesn't realize what the letter means, but we do, and if the rascal has told them that it was taken away from him they would realize at once that they were up against it, and hard!"

"Well, you haven't told me the whole story," he said, with a suggestion of being offended in his tone. "So I can't give you my advice as I would be glad to do if you had taken me into your confidence."

"You'll know it all pretty soon, Niles," said Charlie. "Don't think you're being slighted— you're not. I know just how valuable you are to

4—C7

us, and that we couldn't get along without you.
And, what's more, I'll say that I never saw a case
handled better than this one. You're all right.
Don't worry; I don't care much if they do know.
It's too late for them to do anything now. I'm
going to run back to the hotel. I've got to
get a few papers from my room. Then I'll be
back.''

Leaving Niles with little ceremony, he hurried
back to the hotel, and went directly to his room,
without telling anyone where he was going. As
he passed through the lobby the clerk happened
to be busy and did not see him, and, since his room
was on the second floor, he did not wait for the
elevator, but walked up. Seemingly, the only person who was interested in his movements was the
sinister, black-browed man who had been talking
so earnestly with Holmes in the courtroom half an
hour before. And Charlie, in a great hurry, paid
no attention to him—probably did not even know
that he was in the hotel.

With the man, however, matters were very different. He watched Charlie go up the stairs with the keen eyes of a hawk; and, a minute later, followed him up. And when, ten minutes after he had entered his room, Charlie opened the door to come out, he was met with a sharp blow on the chest that staggered him and sent him reeling back into his room.

In an instant the sinister man he had dismissed so readily from his mind when he had seen him talking with Holmes was on him, the door closing as he flung himself through it, and Charlie, taken completely by surprise, was overpowered before he could even begin to put up any sort of resistance.

Even his belated impulse to call for help came too late. A gag was thrust into his mouth as he was about to open it, and then, with no pains to be gentle, his assailant produced stout cord from his pocket and tied him securely to the bed.

While he was thus rendering Charlie impotent to obstruct him in any way the ruffian said nothing whatever. Now, however, standing off a minute, and looking at his victim with much satisfaction, he broke his silence.

"Trussed up as neat as a turkey for Thanksgiving," he said, in a hoarse whisper that seemed to be his natural speaking voice. "You won't do any more damage, I guess."

And then Charlie, who had been bewildered by this attack, realized at last its meaning. For his assailant came close to him, began to search his pockets, and, in a moment, drew out, with a cry of triumph, the precious letter from Holmes to the gypsy—the letter without which the whole case against Holmes was bound to collapse!

Charlie struggled insanely for a moment, but then suddenly he grew quiet. For his eyes had happened to wander toward the window, which the thief, with the carelessness for details that has caused the downfall of so many of his kind, had left uncovered. And, peering straight at him from a window across a small light shaft, he saw Bessie King. He was longing to communicate with her when the thief suddenly addressed him again.

"Say, bo," he said, in the same hoarse whisper, "I ain't got nuttin' against you, see? If youse wants this here writin', you can have it—if youse is willin' to pay more fer it than the other guy!"

He looked greedily at Charlie, and, though the lawyer understood thoroughly that the man was only trying to add to the money that Holmes had promised him, and would probably not give up the paper, no matter how much was offered, he jumped at the chance to gain time. Bessie had disappeared, and he was sure that she had gone for help. If he could hold the robber for a few minutes he might beat him yet.

To talk with the gag in his mouth was, of course, impossible, and he managed to lift his bound hands toward his mouth to remind the robber of this.

"Say, that's right," said the thief. "Here, I'll ease youse a bit so youse can talk. But no tricks, mind!"

"How much do you want?" gasped Charlie,

when he was able to speak. The man stood over
him, ready to silence any attempt to cry out, and
he knew that it would be useless to call.

"How much you got? I don't mean in your
clothes, but what youse has got salted away in
your room," asked the thief. "I ain't got time
to look for it or I'd leave you tied up," he added,
with a leer.

"You've got something to sell, so name your
price," said Charlie, still trying to kill time.
"That's for you to do. What does the other side
offer you?"

"Gimme two hundred bucks!" suggested the
robber.

"That's a lot of money," said Charlie, pre-
tending to hesitate. "I might give it to you, but
I haven't got it here. I could get it for you or
give you a check——"

"Cash—and cash down!" leered the robber.
"An' say, if youse thinks some of them dames
youse is workin' with can help youse out of this
hole, guess again. They're all locked up, same as

you—from the outside. And there ain't no telephones in the rooms in this hotel.''

For a moment Charlie's heart sank. If this was true, even though she realized his danger, Bessie could not help him. He did not know what to do, or what to say. But, fortunately for him, he was spared from deciding. For there was a sudden crash at the door, and in a moment it gave way before the onslaught of the proprietor, two or three clerks, and a couple of stout porters. In a second the robber was overpowered and a prisoner, and then Charlie saw Bessie, her eyes alight with eagerness, in the background.

"I climbed down the waterspout!" she cried. "I knew I had to get them to help you!"

CHAPTER VII

BACK AT LONG LAKE

"Why, Bessie's a regular brick!" said Charlie, as they sat at dinner that night. Eleanor and the two girls were going back to Long Lake on the first train in the morning, and they were celebrating with the best dinner the town of Hamilton could afford. "I told you I needed a nurse, Nell, and here one of you had to save me for the second time since I came here to look after you!"

"That man was terribly clever," said Eleanor, gravely. "I never even knew I was locked in —I was let out before I had had a chance to find it out for myself."

"Bessie and I didn't know it, either, until she saw him tying Mr. Jamieson up," said Dolly. "We'd have found it out as soon as we wanted to leave the room to go down for lunch, of course, but he was so quiet about locking us in that neither of us heard him at all."

105

"He was just a little bit too clever," said
Charlie. "If he hadn't been so anxious to make
a little more money out of me, he would have got
clean away and given that paper to Holmes."

"Not getting it seemed to upset Mr. Holmes a
good deal, didn't it?" laughed Eleanor. "Is it
true that he left town by the first train after he
heard that the letter had been found when they
searched that wretched man?"

"Quite true," said Charlie, happily.

"Just what did happen in court this afternoon?"
asked Dolly. "I thought we were going to be witnesses and have all sorts of fun. And now it's
all over and our trip down here has just been
wasted!"

"Why, Holmes's lawyer, Curtin, threw up the
case as soon as he heard about that letter, Dolly.
There wasn't anything else for him to do. With
that, added to the stories you two girls had to
tell, there wasn't any way of getting those gypsies off."

"Are they going to send them to prison?"

"John will go to jail for six months. He's the one who actually carried Dolly off, you know. As for Peter and Lolla, who helped him, they get off easily. They were sentenced, too, but the judge suspended sentence. If they forget, and do anything more that's wrong, they'll have to serve out their term."

"I'm very glad," said Eleanor. "Poor souls! I don't believe they understood what a dreadful thing they were doing."

"It was a good thing for them they decided to plead guilty and take their medicine," said Charlie. "Or, I should say, it's a good thing that Curtin decided it for them. Don't worry about them any more. Holmes will have to pay John a good deal of money when he comes out of jail to make him keep quiet—if he manages, first, to shut up the people here, so that the whole story doesn't come out."

"Can he do that, now that they've seen that letter?"

"I'm half afraid he can. He's got a tremendous

lot of money, you see, and this is a time when he naturally wouldn't hesitate much about spending it. And I don't know that it's such a bad thing. It gives us a starting point, you see. And if the thing isn't made public, he may get more reckless, and give us another chance to land him where he belongs, and that's in the penitentiary. He's cleared out now and we couldn't persuade these people to go after him, even if it was worth while, which I don't believe it is.''

"How on earth did you get down?'' Eleanor asked Bessie.

"Oh, I saw there wasn't anything else to do,'' said Bessie, modestly. "If you could have seen that man's face! I was terribly frightened. I didn't know what he might be going to do to Mr. Jamieson, so I just knew I had to get help. And I was afraid to call out of the window.''

"Why? Someone would have been sure to hear you,'' said Eleanor.

"Because I thought the only person who was absolutely sure to hear me was that man who was tying Mr. Jamieson up. And I didn't know what he would do, but I was afraid he might do something dreadful right away if I called out and he knew that he was being watched.''

''You're all right, Bessie!'' said Jamieson, admiringly. ''Was it very hard, going down the waterspout?''

''No, it really wasn't. Dolly was afraid I was going to fall, and she wanted to go herself. But I said I had seen it, and made the plan, and so I had a right to be the one to go. It really wasn't so far.''

''Far enough,'' said Jamieson, grimly. ''You might easily have broken your neck, climbing down three flights that way.''

''Oh, but it wasn't three! It was only one. You see, there was a balcony outside the window, and on the next floor there was another, and I thought that window was pretty sure to be open. It was, so I got inside, and then I found the room I was in was empty, and the door was open, so all I had to do was to walk down the stairs and tell the man-

ager. They all came up and, well, you know what
happened then yourself.''

"I certainly do!" said Jamieson. "And I don't
think I'm likely to forget it very soon, either.
That was a pretty tough character. I'll remember
his face, all right.''

"Well," said Eleanor, happily, "all's well that
ends well, they say. I really believe Dolly had
the worst time, when you think about it. She
had to watch Bessie climbing down that waterspout.''

"That was dreadful," said Dolly, shuddering
at the memory. "But I think it was much worse
for Mr. Jamieson and Bessie than for me.''

"Bessie was so busy getting down that I don't
believe she had much time to think about the danger," said Eleanor. "And Mr. Jamieson didn't
know her door was locked, so he had the relief
of thinking that she'd been able to get help in
just an ordinary fashion. Of course, if he or I
had known what a risk she was running we'd have
been half wild with anxiety about her. So you

see it really was hard for you not to scream or do anything to startle that man.''

"That was what I was afraid of most," said Bessie. "I don't know what I'd have done if Dolly had screamed.''

"You needn't have been afraid! I was too frightened even to open my mouth," said Dolly, honestly. "I couldn't have uttered a sound, no matter what depended on it, until I saw you were all right. And then I just slumped down and laughed—as if there was something funny.''

"Well, we can all laugh at it now," said Eleanor. "Are you going back to the city to-night, Charlie?''

"No, I guess I'll be held up here until about noon to-morrow," he answered. "I've got to appear against that poor chap, and there are one or two other matters I want to attend to while I'm here. I'll see you on your train in the morning, and I'll try to look out for myself when you're gone.''

It was an enthusiastic and eagerly curious crowd

of girls that welcomed them back to Long Lake·
the next day when, in the middle of the morning,
the well-remembered camp appeared. Miss Drew,
who had taken Eleanor's place as Guardian,
laughed as she greeted her friend.

"I don't know how you do it, Nell," she said.
"I never saw anything like these girls of yours.
They did their best not to let me know, but I managed to find out, without their knowing it, that
you did about everything in a different way from
mine—and a much better way."

"Nonsense!" said Eleanor. "I've made a few
changes in the theoretical rules of the Camp Fire.
All Guardians are allowed to do that, you know.
But it's only because they seemed to suit us a
little better—my ideas, I mean."

"You know," said Anna Drew, thoughtfully,
"I think that's the very best thing about the
Camp Fire. It doesn't hold you down to hard
and fast rules that have got to be followed just
so."

"If it did, it would defeat its own purposes,"

IN THE MOUNTAINS   113

said Eleanor. "What we want to do—and it's for Guardians, if they're youngsters like you and me, as well as for the girls—is to train ourselves to attend to our jobs properly."

"Why, what jobs do you mean?"

"The job every girl ought to get sooner or later —running a home. It's a lot more of a job, and a lot more difficult, and important, too, than waiting on people in a shop, or being a stenographer, and yet no one ever thinks an awful lot about it before it comes along."

"That's so, Nell. I never thought of it just that way. But you're right. We get married, and a whole lot of us don't have any idea at all of how to look after a house."

"It isn't fair to the men who marry us. Marriage is supposed to be a partnership—husband and wife as partners. But if the man knew as little about his part of the job as the woman generally does about hers when she gets married, most married couples would be in the poorhouse in a year."

4—C8

"That sounds old-fashioned, but I don't believe it is, somehow."

"It certainly is not. It's what I try to keep in mind. That's why we don't go in much for talking about votes for women. I'm not saying we ought not to vote, or that we ought to. But I do think there are a lot of things we ought to think about first. Times have changed a lot, but after all women and men don't change so very much. Or, at least, they ought not to change."

"I think I see what you're driving at. You mean that your great grandmother and mine probably spun cloth and made clothes for themselves and most of the family, and did all sorts of other things that we never think of doing?"

"Yes. And I don't mean that we ought to go back to that. A man can buy a better shirt in a shop now for less money than you or I would have to spend in making him one. But there are plenty of other things we could do in a house that we never seem to think of, somehow."

"I don't see how you think of all that! I thought

I'd spent a lot of time studying the Camp Fire, but I never got hold of those ideas.''

''Oh, they're not all mine—not a bit of it! You ought to talk to Mrs. Chester, our Chief Guardian. She'd make you think, and she'd make you believe you were doing it all by yourself, too.''

''Yes, she's wonderful. I don't know her very well, but I hope to see more of her this winter. I want to be Guardian of a Camp Fire of my own. I've had just enough of the work, substituting for other girls, to want to spend a lot more time at it.''

''You'll get the chance all right—don't worry about that! It's Guardians we need more than anything else. It isn't as easy as you would think to get girls and women who've got the patience and the time for the work. But that's chiefly because they don't know how fascinating it is, and how much more fun there is in doing it than in spending all your time going about having what people call a 'good time.' I've never had such a good time in my life as since we got up this Manasquan Camp Fire.''

"Well, I wish I could stay with you, and go on this wonderful tramp with you. But I've got a lot of girls coming up to visit me, and I've simply got to be there to entertain them. So if you're really going to stay, and don't need me any more, I'll have to be getting Andrew to take me back home again.''

"I wish you could stay, too, but if you can't, you can't. I'm ever so grateful to you for coming. I can tell you right now that there aren't many people I'd trust my girls to, as I did with you!''

"I know it's a compliment, Nell, so you needn't talk about gratitude. I'm the one to be grateful, I'm sure. The more experience I get before I'm a regular Guardian myself, the better chance I'll have to make good when the time comes.''

"I'm ever so glad you feel that way about it, Anna. You know, there are ever and ever so many girls who could do the work, and won't try. I'm not sure that it's so much 'won't' as—oh, I don't know! I think they're afraid—they haven't any confidence in themselves. They think it would be absurd for them to try to direct others. I felt that way myself."

"Nearly everyone who is at all likely to make good does, Anna. That's the strangest part of it. When I hear a girl talking about how easy it is to be a good Guardian, and how sure she is that she'll make good, I'm always afraid she's going to fail. If you make the girls understand they've got to help you, and that you know that if they don't you won't be able to succeed, you get them ever so much more interested."

"That's easy to understand. It makes them feel that they really do have a part in the work. I noticed that about your girls, particularly, Nell. They seemed to feel that they were all a part of the Camp Fire."

"Well, that's the spirit I've always tried to put into them. I'm very glad if I've really succeeded in doing it. It was a good deal of a trust for me, as well as for them—leaving them to you. It shows, I think, that the Camp Fire is in good shape and able to get along, not exactly by itself, but under different conditions. I might easily have to leave them, you know, and if they couldn't go right ahead under another Guardian, I'd feel that my work had been, in a way, at least, a failure.''

"All ready, Miss Drew!'' called old Andrew, and then the girls gathered on the beach and sung the Wo-he-lo song as the boat glided off.

Eleanor welcomed the quiet days that followed, during which she completed the plans for the field day in which the Boy Scouts were also to take part, and for the long tramp she planned as the chief event of the summer for her girls.

"It seems sort of slow, now that those gypsies have gone, and there's no one to make trouble for us,'' Dolly complained. But Bessie and Zara, who heard her, only laughed at her.

"You'd better be careful,'' said Zara. "First thing you know you'll be starting some new trouble.''

"She's right,'' said Bessie. "You said when we

got away from that gypsy that you'd had enough
excitement for awhile, Dolly."

"Oh, well," Dolly pouted, "it is slow up here—
no place to buy soda, no moving picture shows—
nothing!"

"I call the swimming and the walks pretty exciting," said Zara. "I'm really learning. I went
about twenfy yards this afternoon."

"But I know how to swim, and one walk is just
like another," said Dolly.

"Well, we'll have the field day pretty soon, and
then, after that, we'll start on our long walk.
There'll be plenty of excitement then, and one walk
won't be just like another. I bet you'll be wishing
for a train before we're down in the valley again."

CHAPTER VIII

A NOVEL RACE

The morning of the long-awaited field day dawned clear and bright. The camp was stirring with the first rays of the rising sun, that gilded the tree tops to the east, and painted the surface of the lake, smooth as a mirror, with a hundred hues. The day promised to be hot in the open, but there was no danger of great heat on the march, which was entirely through the woods.

"We won't worry about how hot it's going to be under the sun," said Eleanor Mercer as the girls sat at their early breakfast.

"No. Our work is under the trees, until we get to the camping spot," said Margery Burton.

"Now here's the plan of campaign," said Eleanor. "I am going to send two girls ahead to build the fire. That's the most important thing, really—to get the fire started."

"We can't use matches, can we?" asked Zara.

"No, the fire must be made Indian fashion, with two sticks. But we all know how to do that, I think. The idea of sending two girls ahead is to have that part of the work done when the main body reaches our camping ground."

"Where is that? We can know now, can't we, Wanaka?" asked Margery.

"Yes, it's all right to tell you now. You know those twin peaks beyond Little Bear Lake—North Peak and South Peak?"

"Yes," came the answer, in chorus.

"Well, our place is on North Peak, and Mr. Hastings will take his Scouts to South Peak. The trails are different, but they're the same length."

"Why was that kept such a secret?" asked Bessie.

"Because Mr. Hastings and I decided that it would be fairer if there was no chance at all to go over the trail first and learn all about it. Then there was the chance that if either party thought of it they could locate kindling wood and fallen wood that could be used for the fire-making. On

a regular hike, you see, you would go to a place
that was entirely strange, and it seemed better
to keep things just as near to regular hiking conditions as we could.''

"Oh, I see! And that's a good idea, too. It's
just as fair for one as for the other, then.''

"Who are going to be the two girls to go ahead?
And why can't we all get there at the same time?''
asked Dolly.

"One question at a time,'' said Eleanor, with a
laugh. "I'll answer the second one first. We've
got to carry all the things we need for making
camp and getting a meal cooked. So if we send
out two girls ahead, with nothing to carry, they
can make much better time than those who have
the heavy loads.''

"Will they do the same thing?'' asked Zara.
"The Boy Scouts, I mean?''

Eleanor smiled.

"Ah, I don't know,'' she said. "They will if
Mr. Hastings thinks of it, I'm sure, because it
would be a good move in a race.''

"Is it quite fair in case they don't happen to think of it?" asked Margery, doubtfully.

"Why not? This isn't just like a foot-race. It isn't altogether a matter of speed and strength, or even of endurance—"

"I should hope not!" declared Dolly. "If it was, what chance would we have against those boys?"

"Suppose we found some new way of rubbing sticks that would make fire quicker than the regular way, it would be fair to use that, wouldn't it, Margery?" asked Bessie.

"That's the idea. Bessie's right, Margery," said Eleanor. "We have a perfect right, and so have they, to employ any time-saving idea we happen to get hold of. And I'm quite sure this is a good one, and that Mr. Hastings will think of it, too."

"Well, I hope he doesn't do anything of the sort!" said Margery, wholly converted and now enthusiastic for the plan.

"You haven't told us yet who is to go ahead,"

said Dolly. "I'm just crazy to be one of the two—"

"We all are! Who wouldn't like to get out of carrying a load?" cried two or three girls in chorus.

Eleanor laughed at the eagerness they displayed.

"It won't be all fun for the pathfinders, as we'll call them," she said. "They've got a lot of responsibility, you see."

"What sort of responsibility?" asked Margery. "All they've got to do is to go just as fast as they can and make a fire when they get to the peak."

"That isn't all they've got to do, though. They've got to make a smoke signal, for one thing, by stopping the smoke with a blanket, and then letting it rise, straight up, three times. And they've got to go to work and get enough wood to keep the fire going, as soon as they've lighted it."

"But they'll be able to go along ever so easily on the trail!"

"It isn't a very well marked trail. Neither of

the trails to the peak is, for that matter. And the pathfinders, if they find they're in any danger of making a wrong turn, must make a sign for us who follow. That might easily save us a good many minutes in getting there. So you see it isn't quite as easy as you thought. Now, I'll call for volunteers. Who wants to join the pathfinders?''

Every girl there put up her hand at once, amid a chorus of laughs and jesting remarks.

''Heavens! Well, you can't all be pathfinders, or there'd be no one to carry the dinner! We'll have to figure out some way of picking out two, because that's all there can be.''

''We might draw lots,'' said Margery.

' ''I don't like that idea much,'' said Eleanor. ''If you're all so anxious to go, we ought to make it a reward of some sort—a prize. It's too bad I didn't think of it earlier, because then we could have had a really good competition.''

She frowned thoughtfully for a moment.

''I know what we'll do,'' she said. ''There are just eight of you, and we'll divide all the dishes from breakfast into eight even piles. We can do that easily. Then you shall all start together—"

"Oh, that's good!" said Dolly. "And the ones who finish first will be pathfinders?"

"Yes, those who finish first, and put their dishes away properly, Dolly—not just finish washing and drying. I'll be the judge. Come on, Margery, we'll arrange the piles."

So the arrangements were made, and then, with each girl standing over her own pile of dishes, they waited eagerly for the word.

"I'll start you," laughed Eleanor. "Now, are you ready? Take dishes—wash!"

And at once there was a great splashing and commotion. But Eleanor broke in with a laugh.

"Time!" she called. "Stop washing!"

Everyone stopped, and looked at her curiously.

"Here's a rule," she said. "I only just thought of it. Anyone who breaks a dish is out of the race, even if she finishes five minutes ahead of the next girl. Understand?"

"Yes," they cried.

"All right. Dolly, you kept on washing for nearly half a minute after the others had stopped. When I give them the word to start again, don't you do it. I'll give you a starting signal of your own. You, too, Mary King! I'll call your names when you two are to start."

Then they bent to their piles again, and waited for Eleanor's "Ready? Wash!"

Dolly and Mary King, forced to restore the time they had unwittingly stolen from the others, waited as patiently as they could until they heard "Now, Dolly!" and after a moment more, "All right, Mary!"

"Oh, this is fine sport!" cried Dolly, washing with an energy she had never displayed before. "I think we ought to have races like this ever so often. They're much better fun than most of the games we play!"

"Anything that makes you act as if you liked work is a fine little idea, Dolly," said Margery. "But I haven't got time to talk—I've got to wash.

I never thought anyone could wash dishes as fast
as you're doing it!"

"I'm in practice," laughed Dolly. "I hate them
so, that I'm always trying to get them done just as
quickly as I can."

And a moment later Dolly, to the general surprise, had put away her last dish, an easy winner.

It was plain to her in a moment that the struggle, now that she was out of it, would be between
Margery and Bessie. They had finished washing
almost at the same moment, with Margery perhaps
a couple of spoons ahead.

"Hurry, Bessie, do hurry!" pleaded Dolly.
"We've done so much together up here, we ought
to be pathfinders together, too. Can't I help her,
Miss Eleanor?"

"No, that wouldn't be fair, Dolly," laughed
Eleanor. "Each one has got to win or lose on
her own merits in this race."

Bessie smiled as she heard Dolly's impulsive appeal. She wanted to win, too, because it was impossible for her to engage in any contest without

4—C9

wanting to come out ahead, or as far ahead as she could. This time, of course, second place was all she could hope for, but she was not one of those people who, if the chief prize is beyond their reach, relax their efforts to do as well as they can.

As she finished wiping each dish dry she arranged it, stacking her dishes in order of their size, so that they could all be carried easily to the tent where they were to be laid away.

Margery, on the other hand, grew nervous as she neared the end. Once a plate slipped through her hand, but, fortunately, her cry of dismay as it fell was premature, for it did not break. But she was putting her dishes down anywhere, without regard for their size or for convenience in carrying them, and as a result, though she had finished the actual drying nearly a minute before Bessie, she was still frantically gathering her piled dishes together in her arms when Bessie wiped the last spoon.

Then, without haste, Bessie picked up her whole pile, and, starting before Margery, walked care-

fully over to the tent. She put away her last dish
before Margery was half done, and the contest was
over.

"Go on, girls!" cried Eleanor, as she saw that
interest was slackening with the choice of the sec
ond pathfinder. "You don't want to be last, do
you? I should think you'd all want to avoid
that!"

The reminder was enough, and the others were
soon busily finishing their tasks. Zara was fourth,
right after Margery, and then there was a wild
scramble among the last four. They finished
almost together, and Eleanor, with a laugh, had
to declare that there was a tie for sixth, seventh
and eighth places.

"So no one was really last!" she declared, merrily. "My, but that was good fun! It certainly
was, if you enjoyed racing half as much as I did
watching you! It's a pity we never thought of
that before."

"I'll beat you next time, you two!" vowed the
panting Margery, shaking her first in mock anger

at Bessie and Dolly. "More haste, less speed!
That's what beat me! But I'll know better next
time."

"We'll have a team race some time," said
Eleanor. "Two teams of four—that ought to be
good fun. Ou, there are lots of ways of having a
good time if you only think of them!"

Then she clapped her hands as a sign for attention.

"Now we've got to take our fun for the rest of
the day more seriously," she said. "You girls
will have to take your fire-making sticks, and an
old blanket. You understand how to make smoke
signals, don't you?"

"Yes, indeed!" cried Dolly and Bessie, in one
breath.

"All right, then. How will you make signs to
show us which way to go?"

"With a hatchet. We'll blaze the trees," suggested Bessie. "Then you'll be sure to see it.
There's no way that a sign like that can be blown
away, or get moved by accident. With the thin

end of the blaze in the direction you are to take, if there's a choice.''

''All right. Hatchet, old blanket, fire-making sticks. You'd better carry water bottles, for you'll be thirsty on the way.''

''Why, we'll find plenty of water. There must be springs!'' Dolly protested.

''Undoubtedly; but you don't know just where they are, and you'd waste time looking for them. If you have your water bottles, with a little bit of lemon juice in the water, you can have a drink wherever you like.''

''I like the taste of lemon juice, too.''

''It isn't only because you like it that it's a good thing to have it, but it will quench your thirst better than plain water, and it will make your water last better, too, because you don't need to drink so much of it.''

''It's fine if you're hot, too,'' said Margery, approvingly. ''A little lemon water will cool you off better than half a dozen of those ice-cream sodas you're so fond of, Dolly.''

Dolly made a face at her.

"I think it's mean of you to tease me about soda when you know I can't have it, no matter how much I want it," she said. "But I don't care, really. I wouldn't have an ice-cream soda now, if I had a pocket full of money and I could get one by going across the street!"

Eleanor smiled at her.

"What a reckless promise! Only you know you are perfectly safe," she said, half mockingly.

"I really mean it," protested Dolly. "I'm going to swear off—for a long time, anyhow. Bessie and Zara and I are going to try to get enough honor beads to be Fire-Makers as soon as we get back to the city, and that's one of the ways I'm going to try."

"Then you've started already?" said Eleanor.

"No, not yet," said Dolly. "I'm going to wait—"

A shout of laughter interrupted her.

"Oh, yes, we know! Until you have just one or two last ones—"

Dolly flushed dangerously for a moment. But her new control over herself, that she was fighting so hard to maintain, saved her from the sharp reply that was on her tongue.

"You might let me finish," she said. "If I swore off now I suppose the time while we're here would count toward an honor bead, but what's the use of swearing off something I can't get, anyhow? I'm going to swear off the first time I see a soda fountain!"

"Good for you, Dolly!" exclaimed Eleanor, heartily. "That's the right spirit."

CHAPTER IX

THE PATHFINDERS

It did not take the two pathfinders long to get so far ahead of the main party that they were out of sight and almost out of hearing. The girls who carried the necessary provisions and utensils, however, made their way light by singing Camp Fire songs as they walked, and their voices echoed through the woods.

"This is great! Oh, I love it!" said Dolly, happily. "I'm so glad you beat Margery, Bessie!"

"I thought you liked Margery, Dolly?"

"I do, but you're my very dearest chum, Bessie! I think Margery's great, but she is just a little bit superior, sometimes. I expect I deserve it when she gives me a lecture, but I like you because you don't preach, though you're just as good as she is any day in the week!"

137

"I'll probably lecture you some time, Dolly, if I think you need it."

"Go ahead! I don't mind when you do it, or if you do it.' I don't know why, but it's the same way with Miss Eleanor. She's scolded me sometimes, but she isn't a bit like my Aunt Mabel, or the teachers at school."

"How do you mean? They're kind to you, I suppose? It isn't that that makes the difference?"

"No. I don't just know what it is, except that she makes me feel as if I had made her unhappy, and they always talk just as if they thought it was their duty."

"It probably is, Dolly. You ought to have had the sort of scoldings I used to get from Maw Hoover! Then you'd know what a real scolding is like."

"Oh, I just hate that woman, Bessie, for the way she treated you. Don't you hate her, too?"

"I don't know. I used to, but I'm sort of sorry for her, Dolly."

"I don't see why!"

"Well, since I've been away from the farm, I've seen that she didn't have a very much better time than I did. She had to work all day long, and she never got much pleasure."

"That wasn't any excuse for her treating you so badly."

"I think maybe it was, Dolly. I suppose she was nervous, like a whole lot of other women, and she had to have something to wear herself out on. She took things out on me. I'm beginning to think that maybe she wasn't really mad at me when she acted like that. I believe she used to get so upset about things that she had to sort of kick out at whatever was nearest—and it happened to be me."

"Well, I hate her, just the same! You can forgive her if you like, but I'm not going to!"

"It's a good thing she never did anything to you, Dolly. If you hate her like that when you've never even seen her, what would you do if you had some real reason for it?"

Dolly laughed.

"I suppose I am silly," she said, "but I can't help it. I just feel that way, that's all. Do you know what I wish, Bessie?"

"Nothing dreadful, I hope, Dolly."

"She'd think it was, I'm sure—spiteful old cat! I wish you'd find out all about your father and mother, and that they'd not be lost any more."

"Oh, Dolly, so do I! But that wouldn't seem dreadful to Mrs. Hoover, I'm sure. I think she'd be glad enough."

"Let me finish. I wish you'd find them or that they'd find you, and turn out to be ever so rich. They might, you know. It might all be a mistake, or an accident, or something."

"I wouldn't care if they weren't rich, Dolly, if only I knew what had become of them, and why they had to leave me there all that time with the Hoovers."

"I just know there's some good reason, Bessie. You're so nice that you're bound to be happy some time. Of course you'd like to have your father and mother, whether they were rich or not. But wouldn't it be great if they really were rich?"

"I don't know. I don't know what it's like to be rich, Dolly."

"Oh, you could do all sorts of things! You could make them take you back to Hedgeville in an automobile, just for one thing."

"There are lots and lots of places I'd rather go to, Dolly."

"Oh, yes, of course! But think of how every-one would stare at you, and how envious they would be! I bet they'd be sorry then that they weren't nice to you."

Bessie smiled wistfully at the fantastic idea Dolly's lively brain had conjured up.

"It would be fun," she sighed. "They did tease me dreadfully, some of the girls. You see, the Hoovers didn't have so very much money, and my clothes were mostly old things that Maw made over to fit me when she was through with them."

"You could go back in better dresses than any of those Hedgeville girls ever even *saw*, Bessie. And just think of how that horrid Jake Hoover would feel then."

"Oh, well, there's no use thinking about it, Dolly. It won't ever happen. So I shan't be disappointed, anyhow."

"Well, it might happen and I think it's simply great to dream about things that might happen to you. It doesn't do any harm, and it's awfully good fun."

"You do the dreaming, Dolly, and tell me about your dreams. You can do it better than I could. I'm no good at dreaming that way at all."

"All right, that's a bargain. And right now I guess we'd better stop thinking about dreams and attend to pathfinding. Here's a turn. Which way ought we to go?"

"Straight ahead, I'm sure," said Bessie. "See how the trail narrows in the other direction, and it doesn't look as if it had ever been made like the main trail. It's more as if people had just broken through one after another, until a sort of trail was made.''

''Yes, and it isn't straight ahead, either. When there's a big tree in the way, the trail goes around it, and on the regular trail the guides went along a straight line and chopped down trees when they had to.''

''All right. Give me the hatchet, and I'll mark the proper way to go.''

Deftly Bessie, who had had long practice in the use of a hatchet when she lived with the Hoovers, cut off a strip of bark on a tree at the meeting point of the two trails, so that it formed a plain and unmistakable guide to anyone who knew anything at all of woodcraft.

Then they pressed on. They walked fast, and, with nothing to delay them, they made good time, pausing only once in a while to take a sip from their water bottles.

''I can't hear the girls singing any more, can you?'' asked Dolly, presently.

''No,'' said Bessie, pausing to listen. ''I guess

we must be quite a little way ahead of them now. We ought to be, of course.''

''How much sooner than they ought we to reach the peak?''

''That's pretty hard to tell. I don't know how far it is. But I should think we ought to walk about four miles to their three. So if it's ten miles, we ought to be about two miles and a half ahead of them when we get there—and they ought to walk that in about half an hour—say a little more, forty minutes.''

''That would give us plenty of time to get things ready.''

''I should hope so! We really haven't so very much to do when we get there. It's quite an honor for us to be allowed to make the fire, isn't it?''

''Yes, it is. But we won the right to do it, Bessie. You must remember that. And, of course, it isn't like a ceremonial fire.''

''No, but it's a real fire, and an important one. Look! We're beginning to go down hill now.

We'll be climbing again before we get there, though."

"Let's hurry! I'm just crazy to get the fire started. Who is going to make the light?"

"Why, you are, Dolly! You won the dish-washing race, so you've certainly got the right to do that."

"I'll let you do it if you want to, Bessie. I don't care about the old race."

"No. You earned the right. And I believe you can do it better than I can, anyhow."

"It's just a trick, when you once know how. I used to think it was a wonderful thing to do, but it's just as easy as threading a needle."

"That's another thing that isn't easy until you know just how to do it, though."

"I guess that's so. I've seen boys try to do it, ever and ever so many times, and they usually threw the needle and thread away two or three times before they managed it."

"Are we to cook lunch as soon as we all get to the camping spot?"

"I don't think so. It would be too early, you see."

"I guess the fire will be made, though. Do you know what we are going to have?"

"Potatoes. I saw those. And I believe we're going to have a ham, too. And coffee, of course, and a lot of fruit for dessert."

"Well, the ham would take quite a long time to cook. I guess maybe we'd have to start in cooking right away to get finished in time."

"The boys ought to be having just the same sort of meal that we do. Or else it wouldn't be fair, because some things take longer to cook than others, and you can't hurry them, either."

"Oh, I remember now that Miss Eleanor spoke about that. That's one of the rules."

"I believe we're getting near, for the trail is rising pretty sharply now," said Dolly.

"That's so. See how hilly it is getting to be. It's quite clear on top of the peaks, I believe. I wonder if we'll be able to see them on the other peak and if they'll be able to see us?"

"We'll see the smoke, anyhow. There's nearly half a mile between the two peaks, Miss Eleanor said."

"Come on, let's hurry. I'll be dreadfully disappointed if they get their fire started first."

"So will I."

Then the ascent grew so sharp that for a time they needed all their breath for the climb before them. But the prospect of reaching their destination prevented them from being weary; they were too excited by this strange sort of race in which the contestants could not see one another at all.

"I think this is splendid!" panted Bessie. "This being on our honor. Either side could cheat, and the other wouldn't know it—but neither side will."

"Oh, there's no fun in cheating," said Dolly, scornfully. "If I win anything, I want to know I've really won it, not that I got it because I was smarter than someone else that way."

"That's right. Of course it's no fun to cheat!

I always wonder why people who cheat play games at all. I don't believe they really know themselves, or they wouldn't do it.''

Then came the last part of the ascent, and they went at it with a will, though they were ready for a rest. But when they reached the summit, and were able to stand still at last in an open space almost altogether clear of trees they were amply rewarded for all their exertions.

First of all they looked eagerly to the south, toward the peak that was the twin of their own. A happy exclamation burst from them simultaneously.

"No smoke there yet!" cried Bessie.

"We're here in time!" echoed Dolly.

"We mustn't waste any time, though," cried Bessie. "Get your sticks started while I lay a fire, Dolly."

Swiftly Dolly sank to her knees and arranged her fire-making apparatus, the bow, the socket and the drill. Then, while she drew the bow steadily and slowly, making the drill revolve in

the socket which was full of punk, Bessie brought
small, dry sticks and a few leaves, so that when
the spark came in the punk, it would have fuel
upon which to feed.

"There it is—the fire!" cried Dolly. "See how
it runs along in the leaves, Bessie."

First a little glowing ember; then tiny flames,
that crackled and sputtered. And then arose a
wisp of smoke. Carefully Bessie piled on stick
after stick, carefully chosen and well dried by
sun and wind, so that they would burn quickly.

"Oh, the beautiful fire!" cried Dolly. "I do
love it, Bessie. See how it runs along. Really,
it's a splendid fire!"

Merrily it blazed up, bright and clear.

"Now we want some green wood that will make
a smoke," said Dolly. "Here's some. I think
it's burning well enough now, don't you?"

"Yes. Let's make the smoke now."

On went the green, damp wood, resinous and
full of oil. And in a moment a thick smoke hid
the bright, leaping flames.

"Here's the blanket!" cried Dolly. "Catch the other side—now!"

Standing on either side of the fire, the blanket held over it, they dipped it down now, so that the smoke was caught and held under the obstruction. Then they lifted it clear of the fire altogether, and the smoke, released, rose straight up in a long, tall column, that was visible for miles where the trees did not obscure the view. Once and again they repeated this, making three separate columns of smoke before they left the fire to itself.

And still there was no answering smoke from the other peak. The girls had won their race.

"Did the Indians really use those signals?" asked Dolly.

"They certainly did. Out on the plains, you see, smoke like that could be seen for miles and miles. And so, if there were Indians a few miles apart, signals could go very, very quickly for great distances, and they could send messages for hundreds of miles almost as quickly as we can send them now by telegraph.''

Then they piled on more dry wood, and built the fire up so that it was a great, roaring blaze.

''Now we will just find the water. They'll need that for cooking.''

In less than five minutes after they separated to look for the sp..ing they knew was near, Dolly cried out that she had found it. And in the same moment the first smoke rose from South Peak.

CHAPTER X

"There's smoke, Dolly!" cried Bessie, triumphantly. "Oh, but we've beaten them on this! Ours must have gone up twenty minutes before theirs, and they must have been able to see it when they were building their fire, too."

"Good! Oh, we'll take them down a peg or two before we're done today, Bessie!"

"Don't be too confident yet, Dolly. Remember this is only the start. There's ever so much more to be done before we've won."

"I don't care! You and I have done our share, anyhow."

"You certainly have," said Eleanor Mercer's laughing voice. "But Bessie's right; it isn't time to celebrate yet. Come on, now, we're all going to be busy cooking and getting ready to cook."

Dolly and Bessie looked at the girls emerging from the trail in surprised delight.

153

"Well, you've done your share, and more, too." said Bessie. "We thought we came pretty fast, and we didn't expect you for another fifteen minutes, anyway."

"Well, we didn't exactly loiter on the way. I expect we'd all be glad of a chance to rest a little, but that will have to come later. We'll be able to take things easy while we're eating. We're each to allow a full hour for that, you see, no matter when we get ready."

"But if we're ready to start eating first we can start clearing up first, too, can't we?" asked Dolly.

"Certainly! That's the object of hurrying now. When we're ready to sit down we're to make two smokes, and they are to do the same, and again when we've finished, or when our hour is up, at least. We'll keep tabs on one another that way, you see, and each side will know just how much the other has done. There's got to be some such arrangement as that to make it interesting."

"Yes," said Margery Burton. "It wouldn't really seem like a race unless we knew a little something about what the other side was doing, I think."

"Well," said Eleanor, "I see you've got a splendid fire. I'll appoint you chief cook, Margery. You are to be here at the fire, and Zara shall help you."

Zara sprang to attention at once, and she and Margery unwrapped the ham, and got out the big boiler in which it was to be cooked.

"You go and get water, Dolly and Bessie," said Eleanor, then. "There are the buckets. Hurry, now, so that the water can be boiling while the others are fixing the ham."

And so dividing up the tasks that were to be done, she assigned one to each girl. They were all as busy as bees in a moment, and the work flew beneath their accustomed fingers. Miss Eleanor knew the girls thoroughly, and while, as a rule, she saw to it that each girl had to do a certain number of things that did not particularly appeal to her since that made for good discipline, she managed matters differently today.

It was a time to give each girl the sort of work she most enjoyed, and which, therefore, she was likely to do better and more quickly than any of the other girls.

Although a stranger, hearing the singing, and seeing the bustling group of girls without understanding just what they were doing, might have thought he was looking on at a scene of great confusion, order really ruled. Each girl knew exactly what she was to do, and there was no overlapping. Things were done once, and once only, whereas, at the ordinary picnic there are half a dozen willing hands for one task, and none at all for another.

"Too many cooks spoil the broth," says the proverb, and the same rule applies doubly to such meals as the one the girls were so busily preparing. But there was no spoiling here, and in a surprisingly short time most of the girls were able to rest. Places were laid for the meal; plenty

of water had been provided for the cooks, and
there was an ample heap of firewood beside the
fire.

"I'll be ready for dinner when it's time, all
right," said Dolly, sniffing the delicious odor of
the cooking ham as it rose from the fire. "My,
but that smells good!"

"I've heard some people who had to cook meals
say that it spoiled their appetites, and that they
didn't enjoy meals they had to cook themselves,"
said Eleanor. "But I don't believe that applies
to us a bit. You'll be able to eat with the rest
of us, won't you, Margery—you and Zara?"

"I can't speak for Zara," said Margery, laughing. "But I certainly can for myself. Just you
watch me when dinner's ready! Let's start the
coffee, Zara."

A great coffee pot had been brought, and a
muslin sack full of coffee. This sack was now put
in the coffee pot, which was filled with water, and
the pot was set on the fire. There is no better
way of making coffee. The finest French drip

coffee pot in the world can't equal the brew that this simple and old-fashioned method produces. And anyone who has ever tasted really good coffee made in such a fashion will agree that this is so.

"Can those boys really cook, Miss Eleanor?" asked Dolly, looking toward the other peak, whence smoke was rising steadily.

"Can't they, just!" said Eleanor, heartily. "What makes you ask that, Dolly?"

"I don't know. It seems sort of funny for them to be able to do it, that's all. You expect boys to do lots of other things, but cooking seems to be a girl's business."

"Oh, there are lots of times when it's a good thing for a man to be able to cook himself a meal, especially when he's camping out. And they certainly can do it—those Boy Scouts."

"Have you ever tasted any of their cooking?"

"I certainly have. One day I was out for a long tramp near the city, and I managed to lose my way in some fashion. You know some of the roads are pretty lonely, and I managed to go a long way without coming to any sort of a house where I wanted to stop and ask them to let me have something to eat, and I was nearly starved."

"What did you do? Wasn't there even a store where you could have bought something?"

"I didn't find it, if there was. Well, finally I decided to try a short cut through some woods, and I hadn't gone very far when I ran plump into this same troop of Boy Scouts that is on the other peak now!"

"I bet you were glad to see them!"

"Indeed I was. I knew Mr. Hastings, you see, and when I told him I was lost and hungry, he made me sit down right away, and he explained that they were just going to have an early supper."

"That must have been good news!"

"If you knew how hungry I was, you'd believe it. Well, I never have had a meal that tasted half so good. They had crisp bacon, and the most delicious coffee and real biscuit!"

"Biscuit! And had they cooked them them-selves?"

"They certainly had—and they were so good and flaky they fairly melted in my mouth. If you'd tasted that supper you'd never ask again if boys could cook. Those boys over there today will fare just as well as we do ourselves, and they'll have just as good a time getting the meal ready, too."

"I guess they're better able to look after them-selves than most of the boys we know at home."

"Dinner!" cried Margery, then. "Everything else ready? We'll be all ready for you in a jiffy now. The ham's cooked, and so are the potatoes and the corn is all roasted!"

"We're ready whenever you are," said Eleanor, with a glance at the "table." "Dolly, you and Bessie can send up your two smoke signals now. I do believe we're ready to eat before they are!"

"Oh, we're going to beat them all the way!" said Dolly, happily.

Bessie and Dolly, holding the blanket together, wasted no time in making the signal that let those ōn the other peak know that the Camp Fire was ahead in another stage of the race, and, just as the second smoke was made, a faint cheer was carried across the space between the two peaks by the wind, which had shifted.

But it was fully twenty minutes after the girls had begun their meal before two pillars of smoke rose from South Peak as a sign that over there, too, the meal was ready.

"What a shame that we've got to waste a whole hour eating!" said Dolly.

"I don't call it waste. I'm dog-tired," said Margery. "I'm mighty glad to sit down and rest, and I'm mighty hungry, too."

"So'm I," said Bessie. And there were plenty to echo that.

"Well, if no one else will say it, I will," said Margery, presently. "This *is* a good dinner, if I did help cook it."

"No one ever praises your cooking any more; they're too busy eating," said Eleanor. "You established your reputation long ago."

4--C11

"Well, this was the sort of dinner you couldn't spoil," admitted Margery, frankly. "And when people are frightfully hungry, you only waste your time if you do any really fine cooking for them. All they want is food, and they don't care much what it is, or how it's cooked."

"You don't go on that principle, though, Margery. I notice you take just as much trouble with your cooking whether it's likely to be appreciated or not."

"I do that for my own sake because I really enjoy cooking. I know what I'm going to do next year if I can. Teach cooking in the high school. And I think I can get the work, too."

"That's fine, Margery. I know you'll enjoy it."

"I think it will be pretty good fun. You know, it isn't only just the girls in school. A whole lot of older girls come down—brides, and girls who are going to be married. And they are the silliest things, sometimes!"

"Time's nearly up," said Eleanor, looking at her watch. "Bessie, signal four times with the smoke. I want to see if my watch is right by Mr. Hastings'."

Four times the smoke rose, and from the other peak rose two short answering smokes.

"We arranged that signal, you see," said Eleanor. "Now, watch! He'll show the time by his watch. Count the smokes carefully."

First of all came two smokes.

"That's the hour; two o'clock," said Eleanor. "Now count the next lot carefully; that'll be the first digit of the minutes."

Four smoke pillars rose, at regular intervals. And then, after a well-marked pause, six more went up.

"All right," said Eleanor. "Answer with four smokes. That means it was forty-six minutes past two, fourteen minutes to three, when they started signalling. And my watch and his agree exactly, so that's all right."

"We'll have a good lead when we are able to start cleaning up," she continued. "But we can't waste any time. We start at two minutes to three, and you want to remember that they know just how far behind they are, and we won't be able to gain any more time from now on.''

"Why not, Miss Eleanor," asked Margery, "if we've done it so far?"

"It's going to be very different now, Margery. I don't say that they exactly despised us before, but I certainly do believe they underestimated us. They thought they were going to have an easy time, and they probably loafed a little this morning. But now, you see, they know that they're in for a licking if they don't do mighty well, and they'll strain every nerve to beat us.''

"Oh, I suppose so, but we've really got a splendid lead.''

"Yes. And do you know what will happen if we don't look out? We'll be over-confident, just the way they were this morning, and it will have just the same result. In a race, you know, a good runner will very often let a slower one stay ahead until they are near the finish. They call it making the pace. And then, when he gets ready, he goes right by, and wins as he likes.''

But the warning, although Eleanor was sure that it had been needed, seemed to spur the girls on. They were waiting eagerly when she gave the word to start cleaning up, and each girl, her task assigned to her in advance, was at work as soon as the command to go was given.

In no time at all, as it seemed, the dishes were washed. Then Bessie and Dolly, as tenders of the fire, brought buckets of water and poured them over the glowing embers, for the rule of the Camp Fire never to leave a spark of flame behind them in the woods was strictly enforced.

They put the fire out while the others finished packing the things that had to be taken back. All the rubbish had been burned before water was poured on the fire, and when everything was finished and the girls were ready to start the march back to Long Lake there was no sign of their visit except the blackened ring where the fire had burned.

"Zara, I'm going to leave you here as a sentry when we start," said Eleanor. "I'll carry your pack until you join us."

"How long am I to stay?" asked Zara.

"Until you see that their fire is put out. That will mean that they will be ready to start within two minutes, and I want to know just how much of a start we have on the hike home."

"I see. As soon as they put it out I'm to start after you and report?"

"Yes. Here's my watch. Remember the exact time. If they catch up with us, it will be on this hike."

Then they started, singing happily as they went down the hill. The homeward path was easy. Burdens were lighter than they had been on the trip from Long Lake, and the path was mostly down hill. And, moreover, the Camp Fire Girls had the consciousness that, in order to win, they needed only to hold the advantage they had gained.

"Here's Zara!" cried Bessie, who had been looking behind her.

"Good! What time did they put out their fire?" asked Eleanor.

"Just ten minutes after you started," said Zara. "I came as quickly as I could, but you must have been walking fast."

"I told you they'd begin gaining on us," said Eleanor. "See, they picked up ten minutes in clearing up. Come on, now, we must hurry!"

Hurry they did, and when they reached Long Lake there was a brief period of bustle. A new fire had to be made, and they worked with feverish haste. But they were in time. Bessie and Dolly sent up the first smoke signal before any pillar appeared at the other end of the lake. But the margin was small, for the first Boy Scout pillar rose just as they sent up their third!

CHAPTER XI

Two days after the triumph over the Boy Scouts in the test of the trip to Twin Peaks and back, and bidding good-bye regretfully to Long Lake, the girls started on the long tramp that was to take them through the mountains and to the valley below them on the other side.

"I've decided not to try to do any camping on the trip," said Eleanor. "We could have more fun that way, perhaps, but it would mean carrying a lot more, and I think the loads we've got are plenty big enough. I know my own pack is going to feel heavy enough when we strike some of the real climbing later on."

"I should think we could do much better, too, in the way of interesting others in the Camp Fire," said Margery, "if we stay at farm houses or wherever they will take us in. We'll seem to

169

be more among them, and of them. Don't you think so?''

Eleanor smiled at Margery, pleased that she should have guessed one of her reasons for adopting the course she had chosen. She was already thinking seriously of the time when Margery should be able to take her place as a Guardian.

''We won't start tramping right away, you know,'' said Eleanor, as they disembarked from the boats at the end of Long Lake, and started over the trail for the railroad. ''We could tramp through these woods, but it's very slow going, and I feel that we'd do better if we took the train to Crawford, or Lake Dean, where we strike the road through the notch. That will give us a good start, and give us very beautiful and interesting country for our first day's walk.''

''Shall we go on the same railroad we came up on, Miss Eleanor?'' asked Bessie.

''For a little way. We change a few stations further on, though, and get on the line that climbs right up into the mountains. There's no real road that we could follow. We'd have to take wood trails. So we'll save a lot of time here, and have it for the part of the trip where we can have some really good walking.''

The trip to Moose Junction did not take long. The place seemed hardly worthy of its name. There was no imposing station, but only a little wooden shack with a long platform for freight. But at one side of the shack was a train that provoked exclamations of delighted laughter.

''Why, that train hasn't grown up yet!'' exclaimed Dolly, immensely amused when she saw it.

''It's a narrow gauge railroad, you see, Dolly,'' said Eleanor. ''This road is really only used in the summer time. In the winter no one is up here except a few guides who haven't any use for trains, anyhow, and the tracks are covered with snow.''

''I suppose it was cheaper to build than a regular railroad would be?''

''Yes, a good deal cheaper. The cars are

smaller, you see, and then, when they built it, they had a chance to get their cars and engines very cheap. In the old days, a great many railroads were built like this, even the regular roads that were used all the year round. But gradually they were all changed, and the rails were made the same on railroads all over the country, and then these people were able to get their cars and the other things they needed second hand. And it's plenty good enough, of course, for all the use anyone wants to make of this.''

Two puffing little engines were at the head of the two-car train that was waiting at the junction, and, in a little while, after the passengers for Crawford, the terminal station of the road, were all aboard, they pulled out with a great snorting and roaring that amused the girls immensely. But, ridiculous as they looked, the little engines were up to their work, and they took the sharp, steady climb well enough.

"I like this," said Dolly. "It's awfully slow, but you can see the country. On some of those big trains you go so fast you can't see a thing, and this is really worth seeing."

"It certainly is!" exclaimed Bessie, who was gazing raptly out of the window. "Look back there where we came from! Who would ever have thought that there were so many lakes and ponds?"

"We're getting so high above them now that we can see them, Bessie. Look, there's Long Lake, and I do believe I can see Loon Pond, too!"

"I'm sure of it, Dolly. Oh, this is splendid! But we can't see much up ahead, can we?"

"Nothing but trees. It's like the old story of the man who wanted to see a famous forest, and when he was in the very middle of it he said he couldn't see the forest because there were so many trees."

"I've seen mountains before," said Zara. "But they weren't like this. Where I used to live there would be one or two big mountains, but they stood out, and you could see all the way up no matter how close you were."

"Were they all covered with trees, like this?"

"No, not at all. There were lots of little farms, and olive trees, and gardens. And sometimes there would be smoke coming from the top of the mountains."

"You mean the volcanoes, don't you?" said Dolly. "I'd like to see an eruption some time. Like the ones at Vesuvius."

"I never saw one," said Zara, with a shudder. "But I've seen the paths where the lava came down, and the places where people were killed, and where whole villages were wiped out. I'm glad there aren't any around here."

"So is Dolly, Zara," said Bessie, dryly. "She's always wishing for things she doesn't really want at all, because she thinks they would be exciting."

That would have started an argument without fail, if Dolly had not just then had to devote her attention to something that she noticed before anyone else. She sniffed the air that came in through the car windows once or twice.

"I smell smoke," she said. "And look at the sun! It's so funny and red. See, you can look at it without it hurting your eyes at all. And it's a good deal darker, the way it gets before a thunder shower, sometimes."

"She's right," said Bessie. "I believe the woods must be on fire somewhere near here."

"I'm afraid they are," said Eleanor Mercer, who had stopped in the aisle beside them and had overheard Bessie's remark. "But not very near. You know the smoke from a really big forest fire is often carried for miles and miles, if the wind holds steady."

"Well, it can't be so very far—not more than twenty or thirty miles, can it, Miss Eleanor?"

"It's impossible to say, but I have known the smoke from a fire two hundred miles away to make people uncomfortable. They can't smell it, but it darkens the air a little."

"Why, I had no idea of that!"

"Well, here's something stranger yet. I heard you all talking about volcanoes. A good many

years ago there was a frightful eruption in Japan,
or near Japan, rather, when a mountain called
Krakatoa broke out. That was the greatest eruption we know anything about. And a long time
afterward people began to notice that the sunsets
were very beautiful half the way around the world
from it, and no one knew why, until the scientists
explained that it was the dust from the volcano!''

"Well, I hope this fire isn't where we are going!" said Dolly.

"So do I," said Eleanor. "That's the very
first thing I thought of, though. It wouldn't do
to go into a country while the fire was on, because
it might be dangerous and we'd certainly be in
the way of the people who were fighting it, and
that wouldn't be right."

"Whatever should we do, Miss Eleanor? Go
home?"

"Oh, I hardly think it's likely to be as bad as
that. We might have to stay at Crawford for a
day or two, but I was planning to spend tonight
there, anyhow. Some friends of ours have a big

camp on the lake, and they said we could stay, if we wanted to."

"Is it as pretty a place as Long Lake?"

"I think so. But it's quite different. Lake Dean is a great big place, you know. It's more than thirty miles long, and you could put Long Lake into it and never know where it was. But it's very beautiful. And it's the highest big lake anywhere in this part of the world. It's right in the mountains."

"I suppose there will be lots of people there?" asked Dolly.

"Plenty," said Eleanor, smiling back at her. "But we won't have much to do with them, we'll be there such a short time."

"Oh, well, I don't care!" said Dolly, defiantly, as she heard the laugh that greeted Eleanor's answer. "I probably wouldn't like them, anyhow!"

"I really do think it's getting darker. We must be getting nearer to the fire," said Bessie, who had been looking out of the window. "Do

4—C12

you suppose it was some careless campers who started it, Miss Eleanor?''

"That's pretty hard to say. But a whole lot of fires do get started by just such people in the woods. It shows you why we are so careful when we build a fire and have to leave the place.''

In the next hour, as the train still crawled upward, the smoke grew thicker and thicker, until presently it was really like dusk outside the car, and, though it was hot, the windows had to be closed, since the smoke was getting into the eyes of all the passengers and making them smart.

"I used to think a forest fire would be good fun," said Dolly, choking and gasping for breath, "but there isn't any fun about this. And if it's as bad as this here, think of what it must be like for the people who are really close to it.''

"It's about the most serious thing there is.'' said Eleanor, gravely. "There's no fun about a forest fire.''

At Crawford they saw the big lake, but much of its beauty was hidden since it lay under a pall

of heavy smoke. Even then they could see nothing of the fire, but the smoke rose thickly from
the woods to the west of the lake, and they soon
heard, from those about the station, that a great
section of the forest in that direction was ablaze.

"Good thing the lake's in the way," said one
of the station porters. "That's the only thing
that makes us safe. It can't jump water. If it
wasn't for that it'd be on us by morning."

"There are cottages and camps on the other
side of the lake though, aren't there?" asked
Dolly.

"Yes, and they're fighting hard to save them,"
said the porter. "They ain't got much chance,
though, unless the wind shifts and sends the fire
back over the ground it's burned over already.
It's got out of hand, that's what that fire's been
an' gone and done."

"We'll have to stay here until it's out," said
Eleanor, with decision. "Our road begins right
up there"—she pointed to the northwest end of
the lake—"and the chances are the fires will be

burning over that way before the night's over. However, I don't believe there'll be a great amount of damage done, if they can save the buildings on the shores of the lake.''

"Why not, Miss Eleanor?" asked Margery. ''It looks like a pretty bad fire.''

"Oh, it is, but there isn't a great deal to burn. About two or three miles back from the lake there's a wide clearing, and the fire must have started this side of that, or it wouldn't have jumped. And it can't have been burning very long, or we'd have had the smoke at Long Lake.''

Then she went off to make some inquiries, and was back in a few minutes.

"Come on, girls,'' she said. "It's only about ten minutes' walk to Camp Sunset, where we are to stay.''

And she led the way down to the lake, and along to a group of buildings made out of rough hewn logs, that stood among trees near the water.

"Oh!" gasped Dolly, when they were inside the main buildings. "They call this a camp!

Electric lights, and it couldn't be better furnished if it were in the city!"

"The Worcesters like to be comfortable," said Eleanor, with a smile, "even when they pretend they're roughing it. It is a beautiful place, though I like our own rough shacks in the Long Lake country better."

"Come on! I want to explore this place, Bessie!" cried Dolly. "May we, Miss Eleanor?"

"Go ahead, but be back in half an hour. We've got to help to get dinner, even if we are in the midst of luxury!"

So off went the two girls, and Dolly, always delighted by anything new, was all over the place in a few minutes.

"Look at those summer houses—places for having tea, I bet," she said. "Hello! Why, there's another camp, just like this!"

Sure enough, through the trees they could see other buildings, all logs outside, but probably all luxury within. And, even while they were looking at them, Dolly suddenly heard her own name.

"Dolly! Dolly Ransom! Is that really you?"

Dolly and Bessie looked up, surprised, for the call came from above and a girl began to climb down from a tree above them, and they saw that she had been hidden on a platform that was covered by leaves and branches.

"Gladys Cooper!" said Dolly. "Well, whoever would have thought of seeing you here?"

"Oh, there are lots of us here!" said Gladys, rushing up to Dolly as soon as she reached the ground, and embracing her. "We're all in a regular camp here, about a dozen of us. We're supposed to do lessons, but I haven't looked at a book since I've been here, and I don't believe any of the other girls have, either!"

"Oh," said Dolly, suddenly remembering Bessie. "This is Bessie King, Gladys. And this is my friend Gladys Cooper, Bessie. We used to go to school together before her parents sent her off to boarding-school."

Suddenly Gladys broke into a roar of laughter.

"Oh, this is rich!" she exclaimed. "I forgot

—why, you must be one of the Camp Fire Girls
who are coming here, aren't you, Dolly?"

"I certainly am—and Bessie's another," said
Dolly, a little resentfully. "Why are you laughing?"

"Oh, it seems so funny for you to belong! None
of our crowd do, you know, except you. We were
furious when we heard you were coming. We
couldn't see why the Worcesters let you people
have the camp. But you'll spend all your time
with us, won't you, Dolly? And"—she seemed
to remember Bessie suddenly—"bring your friend
along, sometimes."

"Indeed, and I'll stay with my own friends!"
she said, flushing hotly.

CHAPTER XII

"Horrid little snob!" commented Dolly, as, with the surprised Bessie following her, she turned on her heel abruptly and left Gladys Cooper standing and looking after her.

"Why, Dolly! What's the matter? And why did she talk that way about the Camp Fire Girls?"

"Because she's just what I called her—a snob! She thinks that because her father has lots of money, and they can do whatever they like that she and her family are better than almost anyone else. And she and her nasty crowd think the Camp Fire Girls are common because some of us work for a living!"

Dolly's honest anger was very different from the petulance that she had sometimes displayed, as on the occasion when she had been jealous of poor Bessie. And Bessie recognized the difference. It seemed to reveal a new side of Dolly's complex character, the side that was loyal and fine. Dolly was not resenting any injury, real or fancied, to herself now; the insult was to her friends, and Bessie realized that she had never before seen Dolly really angry.

"As if I'd leave you girls and stay with them while we're here!" cried Dolly. "I can just see myself! They'd want to know if I didn't think Mary Smith's new dress was perfectly horrid, and if I said I did, they'd go and tell her, and try to make trouble. Oh, I know them—they're just a lot of cats!"

"Oh, don't you think you may be hard on her, Dolly?" asked Bessie. Secretly she didn't think so; she thought Gladys Cooper was probably just what Dolly had called her. But it seemed to her that she ought to keep Dolly from quarreling with an old friend if she could. "Maybe she just wanted to see you, and she knew you, and didn't know the rest of us."

"Oh, nonsense, Bessie! You're always trying

to make people out better than they are. I don't know these girls who are up here with her, but she'd say she knew me, and that we lived in the right sort of street at home, and that her mother and my aunt called on one another, so I'm all right. I know her little ways!''

And Bessie was wise enough to see that to argue with Dolly while she was in such an angry mood would only make matters worse. Bessie loved peace, because, perhaps, she had had so little of it while she lived in Hedgeville with the Hoovers. But Dolly wasn't in a peaceful mood, and words weren't to bring her into one, so Bessie decided to change the subject.

"We'd better hurry back," she said. "I really think it must be almost time to start getting supper ready."

"Good!" said Dolly. "We haven't really come so far, but it's taken us a long time, hasn't it? That old train from Moose Junction is about the pokiest think in the way of a train I ever saw."

So they made their way back to the big building that, as they had already learned, was called the "Living Camp." The sleeping rooms were in other and smaller buildings, that were grouped about the central one, in which were only three rooms, beside the big kitchen, a huge, square hall, with a polished floor, covered with skins instead of rugs, to bear out the idea of a rough woods dwelling, and two smaller rooms that were used as a dining-room and a library.

And, as soon as they arrived, they found that they were not the only ones who had had an encounter with their next door neighbors. Margery Burton was talking excitedly to Eleanor Mercer.

"I didn't know I was on their old land!" she was saying. "And, if I was, I wasn't doing any harm."

"Tell me just what happened, Margery," said Eleanor, quietly.

"Why, I was just walking about, looking around, the way one always does in a new place, and the first thing I knew a girl in a bathing suit came up to me!

"'I beg your pardon,' she said, 'but do you know that you are trespassing?'

"I said I didn't, of course, and she sort of sneered.

"'Well, you know it now, don't you?' she said, as if she was trying to be just as nasty as she could. 'Why don't you go to the land you're allowed to use? I do think when people are getting charity they ought to be careful!'"

"That's another of that crowd of Gladys Cooper's," stormed Dolly. "What did you say, Margery? I hope you gave her just as good as she sent!"

"I was so astonished and so mad I couldn't say a thing," said Margery. "I was afraid to speak—I know I'd have said something that I'd have been sorry for afterward. So I just turned around and walked away from her."

"What did she do? Did she say anything more, Margery?" asked Eleanor, who, plainly, was just as angry as Dolly, though she had better control of her temper.

"No, she just stood there, and as I walked off she laughed, and you never heard such a nasty laugh in your life! I'd have liked to pick up a stone and throw it at her!"

"Good for you! I wish you had!" said Dolly. "It would have served her right—the cat! Bessie and I met one of them, too, but I happened to know her, so she asked me to come and spend all my time with them while we were here! I'm glad I sailed into her. Bessie seemed to think I was wrong, but I'm just glad I did."

Eleanor Mercer looked troubled. She understood better than the girls themselves the reason for what had happened, and it distressed and hurt her. The other girls who had heard Margery's account of her experience were murmuring indignantly among themselves, and Eleanor could see plainly that there was trouble ahead unless she could manage the situation—the hardest that she had yet had to face as a Camp Fire Guardian.

"You say it was Gladys Cooper you saw,

Dolly?'' she said. ''The Gladys Cooper who lives
in Pine Street at home?''

''Yes, that's the one, Miss Eleanor.''

''I'm surprised and sorry to hear it,'' said
Eleanor. ''How does she happen to be there,
Dolly? Do you know? The Coopers haven't any
camp here, I know.''

''Oh, it's a girls' summer camp, Miss Eleanor.
You know the sort. They're run for a lot of rich
girls, whose parents want to get rid of them for
the summer. They're supposed to do some studying, but all they ever really do is to have a good
time. I'd have gone to one this year if I hadn't
joined the Camp Fire Girls instead. Gladys
laughed at me in the city when she heard I was
going to join.''

''Mrs. Cooper wouldn't like it, I know that,''
said Eleanor, thoughtfully. ''She's a charming
woman. She and my mother are great friends,
and I know her very well, too. There's nothing
snobbish about her, though they have so much
money. I remember now; they went to Europe

this summer, and they didn't take Gladys with them.''

"I wish they had!" said Dolly, viciously. "I wish she was anywhere but here."

"Well," said Eleanor, "I'll find out in the morning just where the line comes between the two camps, and we'll have to be careful not to cross it."

"I'm sure none of us want to go into their camp," said Margery. "But there's no fence, and there aren't any signs, so how is one to know?"

"We'll find some way to tell," said Eleanor, decisively. "And we won't give them any chance to make any more trouble. They've got a right to warn us off their property, of course, though they're just trying to be nasty when they do it. But as long as they are within their rights, we can't complain just because they're doing it to be ugly. We mustn't put ourselves in the wrong because nothing would suit them better."

"Oh, I hope we'll be able to get away to-mor-

row!'' said Margery, angrily. "I don't want ever
to see any of them again.''

Eleanor's eyes flashed.

"I've made up my mind to one thing,'' she said.
"We're going to stay here just as long as we like!
I don't intend to be driven away in that fashion.
And I shouldn't wonder if we could start our mis-
sionary work better with them than with any-
one else!''

"That's right—about staying here, I mean!''
said Dolly, enthusiastically. "Why, Margery, if
we ran away now, they'd think they had scared
us off. You wouldn't want that, would you?''

"No, I guess not!'' said Margery. "I hadn't
thought of that. But it's true. It would be giving
them an awful lot of satisfaction, wouldn't it?''

"Understand, Dolly, and the rest of you,'' said
Eleanor, firmly, "I don't mean to have any petty
fighting and quarrelling going on. But I won't
let them think they can make us run away, either.
Pay no attention to them and keep out of their
way, if you can. But we've got just as much right

4—C13

to be here as they have to be in their camp, because we're here as the guests of the Worcesters."

"I know Miss Worcester," said Margery, hotly. "I'll bet she'd be furious if she knew how they were acting."

"She doesn't need to know, though, Margery," said Eleanor. "This is our quarrel, not hers, and I think we can manage to settle it for ourselves. Don't begin thinking about it. Remember that we're in the right. It will help you to keep your tempers. And don't do anything at all to make it seem that we're in the wrong."

"My, but Miss Eleanor was angry!" said Dolly, when she was alone with Bessie after supper, which, despite the unpleasantness caused by the girls next door, had been as jolly as all meals that the Camp Fire Girls ate together. "I'm glad to see that she can get angry; it makes her seem more like a human being."

Bessie laughed.

"She can get angry, all right, Dolly," she said. "I've heard it said that it isn't the person who

never gets angry that ought to be praised; it's
the person with a bad temper who controls it and
never loses it. Miss Eleanor was angry because
she is fond of us and thought those other girls
were being nasty to us. It wasn't to her that
they'd been nasty.''

"No, and just you watch Gladys Cooper if she
gets a chance to see Miss Eleanor! The Mercers
have got just as much money as the Coopers, and
they are in just as good society. But you don't see
Miss Eleanor putting on airs about it! Gladys
would be nice enough to her, you can bet!''

"Dolly, why don't you go over and see Gladys,
if you know her so well? You might be able to
talk to her and make her see that they are in the
wrong.''

"No, thank you, Bessie! I'm no good at that
sort of thing. I'd just get angry again, and make
the trouble worse than ever. If she's got any
sense at all, she must know I'm angry, and why,
and if she wants to be decent she can come over
and see me.''

Nothing more happened that night. The girls, tired from their journey, were glad to tumble into bed early. They all slept in one house, which contained only sleeping rooms, and, because of the smoke, which was still being blown across the lake when they went to bed, windows had to be closed. The house was ventilated by leaving a big door open in the rear and on the side away from the wind and the smoke, and of course all the doors of the sleeping rooms were also left open.

"I'm awfully sorry that smoke is blowing this way," said Dolly. "Look here, Bessie, there's a regular porch running all the way around the house. And do you see these screens that you can let down? I bet they sleep out here."

"They do," said Eleanor. "This sleeping porch arrangement is one of the very best things about this camp, I think. But I don't see how we can use it to-night, for the smoke is much too thick."

So they regretfully closed their windows. And in the morning they found that visitors had been at the house during the night. Every window was firmly closed from the outside, wedges having been driven in in such a fashion that it was impossible to open the windows from within. The doors, too, were barred in some manner.

"That's a joke those girls from the next camp played on us!" cried Dolly, furiously. "Look there! They must have done it. No one else could have managed it."

The house resembled nothing so much as a hive of angry bees. The girls buzzed with indignation, and loud were the threats of vengeance.

"How are we going to get out?" cried Margery, indignantly. "What a wicked thing to do! Suppose the place had caught fire? We might all have been burned up just because of their joke!"

But Bessie had busied herself in seeking a means of escape instead of planning revenge, and now she called out her discovery.

"Here's a little bit of a window, but I think I can get through it," she said, emerging from a closet that no one had noticed. "If you'll boost me up I'm pretty sure I can get out."

"But you'll only be on the porch when you do get out, Bessie," said Dolly.

"I think maybe I can get those wedges out of the windows if I get out there. If I can't, I'm quite sure I can manage to get to the ground and get help. You see, everything downstairs is barred the same way. I don't see how they could have done all that without our hearing them."

"We were sleeping pretty soundly, Bessie," said Eleanor, her cheeks red with indignation at the trick that had been played upon her girls. "If the windows had been open, they couldn't have done it."

Bessie had hard work getting through the tiny closet window, which had been overlooked by the raiders, but she managed it somehow, and in a moment she was outside. She first ran to the edge of the porch to look around, and, to her anger and surprise, she saw a group of girls, all in bathing suits, watching her and the house. At her appearance a shout of laughter went up, and she recognized Dolly's friend, Gladys Cooper, who was evidently a ringleader in the mischief.

Bessie was sorely tempted to reply, but she realized that she would only be playing into their hand if she seemed to notice them at all, and, going to the other side of the house so that they could not see her, she examined the windows. But she decided very quickly that she could do nothing without tools of some sort, and she had none to work with.

Without any further hesitation, she slipped over the rail of the porch, being still out of sight of the raiders, and went down the pillar, which, being nothing more than a tree with its bark still clinging to it, gave her an easy descent. Once on the ground, her task was easy. She worked very quietly, and in a minute or two she had one of the ground floor windows open. Eleanor Mercer, who had heard her at work, was waiting for her.

"Oh, Miss Eleanor," said Bessie, tensely, "those girls are all around at the other side of the house, watching. They laughed at me like anything when they saw me, and I'm sure they think we'll have to get the guide to let us out."

"Good," said Eleanor, snappily. "Do you think we can get behind them, Bessie?"

"I'm sure we can, if we go out this way and go around through the trees."

So bidding the other girls to stay behind for the moment, Eleanor climbed out, and followed Bessie off the porch and around to the back of the house. They swung around in a wide arc, moving quietly and making as little noise as possible, until they heard laughter in front of them. And a moment later they came around, and faced the astonished raiders.

CHAPTER XIII

A PLAN OF REVENGE

Bessie had to laugh at the sight of Gladys Cooper's face when Dolly's friend saw Miss Eleanor. It fell, and Gladys turned the color of a beet. Evidently she had had no idea that Miss Mercer was with the Camp Fire Girls.

"How do you do, Gladys?" said Eleanor, pleasantly. "Do you know that you are trespassing?"

"The—the Worcesters gave us permission to come on their land whenever we liked," stammered Gladys.

"Yes, when they supposed that they and their guests were to receive the same sort of courtesy from you. But the Worcesters aren't here just now, and I must ask you girls not to come across the line at all, unless you wish to behave in a very different manner."

201

"I—I don't know what you mean, Miss Mercer.
We haven't done anything—"

"That's silly, Gladys. I'm not going to do
anything about it, but I think it would be very
easy to prove that it was you and your friends
who locked us in. Didn't you stop to think of what
would have happened if there had been a fire?"

Gladys grew pale.

"I don't suppose you did," Eleanor went on.
"I don't think you mean to be wicked, any of you.
But just try to think of how you would have felt
if that house had caught fire in the night, and some
of us had been burned to death because we couldn't
get out."

"I didn't—we never thought of that," said
Gladys. "Did we, girls?"

"Well, I don't suppose you did. But that
doesn't excuse the trick you played at all. I'm
not going to say anything more now, but I think
that if you stop to consider yourselves, you'll find
out how mean you were, and what a contemptible
thing you've done."

With heads hanging, and tears in the eyes of some of them, completely crushed by Miss Eleanor's quiet anger as they would not have been had she heaped reproaches upon them, the raiders started to return to their own camp. Eleanor stood aside to let them pass; then, with Bessie, she went back to the camp.

"I hardly think we'll have any more trouble with them," she said.

"I don't see why they dislike us so much," said Bessie. "We haven't done anything to them."

"I don't know how to explain it, Bessie. It isn't American; that's the worst thing about it. But you know that in Europe they have lords and dukes and an aristocracy, don't you? People who think that because they're born in certain families they are better than anyone else?"

"Yes."

"Well, there's a good deal of excuse for people to feel that way over there, because it's their system, and everyone keeps on admitting it, and so making the aristocrats believe it. They're the descendants of men who, hundreds of years ago, really did do great things, and earned certain honors that their children were allowed to inherit.''

"But it isn't the same over here at all, Miss Eleanor.''

"No, and that's just it. But these girls, you see, are all from rich homes. And in this country some people who have a lot of money are trying to make an aristocracy, and the only reason for being in it is having money. That's all wrong, because in this country the best men and women have always said and believed that the only thing that counted was what you were, not what you had.''

"Well, I'm not going to feel bad about them, Miss Eleanor. I guess that if they really were such wonderful people they wouldn't think they had to talk about it all the time, they'd be sure that people would find it out for themselves.''

"You're very sensible, Bessie, and I only hope

the other girls will take it the same way. I really couldn't blame them if they tried to get even in some fashion, but I hope they won't, because I don't want to have any trouble. I'm afraid of Dolly, though.''

''I think Dolly's perfectly fine!'' said Bessie, enthusiastically. ''They were willing to be nice to her, but she stuck to us, and said she wouldn't have anything to do with them.''

''That's what the Camp Fire has done for her, Bessie. I'm afraid that if Dolly hadn't joined us, she'd have been as bad as they are, simply because she wouldn't have stopped to think.''

Bessie considered that thoughtfully for a moment before she answered.

''Well, then, Miss Eleanor,'' she said, finally, ''don't you suppose that if that's so, some of those girls would be just as nice as Dolly, if they belonged to the Camp Fire and really understood it?''

''I'm sure of it, Bessie—just as sure as I can be! And I do wish there was some way of mak-

ing them understand us. I'd rather get girls like
that, who have started wrong, than those who have
always been nice.''

Contrary to Bessie's expectations, when they
reached the Living Camp, Eleanor made no appeal to the girls to refrain from trying to get even
with the raiders. Eleanor knew that if she gave
positive orders that no such attempt was to be
made she would be obeyed, but she felt that this
was an occasion when it would be better to let the
girls have free rein. She knew enough about them
to understand that a smouldering fire of dislike,
were it allowed to burn, would do more harm than
an outbreak, and she could only hope that they
would not take the matter too seriously.

"We're all going in bathing this afternoon after
lunch," said Dolly to Bessie, after breakfast. "I
asked Miss Eleanor, and she said it would be all
right. The water's cold here, but not too cold, and
with this smoke all over everything, I think it will
be better in the water than it would be anywhere
else.''

"The wind hasn't shifted much yet, has it?" said Zara.

"It's shifted, but not altogether the right way," said Bessie. "I think the houses along the lake are all right now, but the wind is blowing the fire in a line parallel with them, you see, and it will burn over a lot more of the woods before they can get it under control."

"Miss Eleanor says we'll have to stay here a couple of days, at least," said Margery. "Girls, what do you think about those cats in the next camp?"

Dolly's teeth snapped viciously.

"I think we ought to get even with them," she said. "Are we going to let them think they can play a trick like that on us and not hear anything at all about it?"

"Oh, what's the use?" said Margery. "I think it would be better if we didn't pay any attention to them at all—just let them think we don't care."

"You were mad enough last night and this

morning, Margery," said Dolly. "You didn't act then as if you didn't care!"

"No, I suppose I didn't. I was as mad as a wet hen, and there's no mistake about that. But, after all, what's the use? I suppose we could put up some sort of game on them, but I'm pretty sure Miss Eleanor wouldn't like it."

"I think you're right," said Bessie. "If we let them alone they'll get tired of trying to do anything nasty to us. You ought to have seen the way they sneaked off when Miss Eleanor spoke to them this morning. They acted just the way I've seen a dog do after it's been whipped."

"Oh, that's all right, too, Bessie," said Dolly. "But that won't last. They probably did feel pretty cheap at first, but when they've had a chance to talk things over, they'll decide that they had the best of us. And I know how Gladys Cooper and the rest of the girls from home will talk. They'll tell about it all over town."

"Let them!" said Margery. "I'm not going to do a thing. And you can't start a war all by yourself, Dolly. If you try it you'll only get into trouble, and be sorry."

"Oh, will I?" said Dolly, defiantly. "Well, I'm not saying a word. But if I see a good chance to get even with them, I'm going to do it—and I won't ask for any help, either! Just you wait!"

"Let's quit scrapping among ourselves, Dolly. Wouldn't they just be tickled to death if they knew we were doing that? Nothing would please them any better."

But even Margery's newly regained patience was to be sorely tried that afternoon, when, after an early lunch, the Camp Fire Girls donned their bathing dresses and went in swimming off the float in front of the Worcester camp.

"Come on, Dolly," she cried. "See that rock out there? I'll race you there and back!"

They went in together, diving so that their heads struck water at just the same moment, while the rest of the girls watched them from the float. On the outward journey they were close together, but they had not more than started back when there

4—C14

was a sudden outburst of laughter from the float
where Gladys Cooper and her friends were watching, and the next moment a white streak shot
through the water, making a terrific din, and kick-
ing up a tremendous lot of spray.

"Whatever is that?" cried Zara.

"A motor boat," said Mary King. "Look at
it go! Why, what are they trying to do?"

The answer to that question was made plain in
a moment. For the motor boat, into which three
or four of the girls from the next camp had leaped,
kept dashing back and forth between the float and
the rock. It raised great waves as it passed, and
made fast swimming, and for that matter, swimming of any sort, almost impossible. Moreover,
it was plain from the laughter of those on board
that their only purpose was to annoy the Camp
Fire Girls and spoil their sport in the water.

Dolly and Margery, exhausted by their struggle
with the waves from the motor boat, struggled
to the float as best they could and came up, drip-
ping and furious.

"See that!" cried Dolly. "They can't be doing that for fun. All they want to do is to bother us. You'd think we had tried to do something mean to them the way they keep on nagging us."

"They certainly seem to be looking for trouble," said Margery. "But let's try not to pay any attention to them, girls."

Margery knew that Eleanor Mercer expected her, so far as she could, to help her on the rare occasions when it was necessary to keep the girls in order, and she realized that she was facing a test of her temper and of her ability to control others. She was anxious to become a Guardian herself, and she now sternly fought down her inclination to agree with Dolly that something should be done to take down the arrogant girls from the next camp, who were so determined to drive them away.

"I shall have to speak to whoever is in charge of those girls," said Eleanor. "I'm quite sure that no teacher would permit such behavior, but

I can imagine that anyone who tried to control those girls would have her hands full, too."

"You bet she would!" said Dolly. "Miss Eleanor, isn't there some way we can get even?"

Eleanor ignored the question. All her sympathies were with Dolly, but she really wanted to avoid trouble, although it was easy to see that unless the other girls changed their tactics, trouble there was bound to be. So she tried to think of what to say to Dolly.

"Try to be patient, Dolly," she said, finally. "Did you ever hear the old saying that pride goes before a fall? I've never known people to act the way those girls are doing without being punished for it in some fashion. If we give them the chance, they'll do something sooner or later that will get them into trouble. And what we want to do, if we can, is to remember that two wrongs don't make a right, and that for us to let ourselves become revengeful won't help matters at all."

But for once Dolly did not seem disposed to take Miss Eleanor's advice as she usually did.

Stealing a look at her chum's face, Bessie knew that Dolly would not rest until she had worked some scheme of revenge, and she felt that she couldn't blame Dolly, either. She could never remember being as angry as these rich, snobbish girls had made her.

Time and again,—every time, in fact, that any of the Camp Fire Girls ventured into the water— the motor boat returned to the charge. Their afternoon's sport in the water, to which all the girls had looked forward so eagerly, was completely spoiled, and the tormentors did not refrain even when Miss Eleanor, who had intended to sit on the float without swimming at all, challenged two or three of the girls to a race. She did that in the hope that the other girls might respect her, but her hope was vain.

To be sure, Gladys Cooper seemed to be a little frightened at the idea of bothering Miss Eleanor.

"Let's keep off until she's through," Bessie heard Gladys saying. "That's Miss Mercer—she knows my mother. We oughn't to bother her.

She comes from one of the best families in town."

But Gladys was laughed down.

"She'll have to suffer for the company she keeps, then," said a big, ugly-looking girl. "Can't play favorites, Gladys! We want to make them see they're not wanted here. My mother only let me come here because we were told this was an exclusive place."

And Miss Eleanor, like the others, was soon forced to beat a retreat to the float. Dolly was strangely silent for the rest of the day. Bessie, watching her anxiously, could tell that Dolly had some trick in her mind, but, try as she would, she could not find out what her plan was.

"No, I won't tell you, Bessie," said Dolly, when her chum finally asked her point-blank what she meant to do. "You're not a sneak, and I'm not afraid of your telling on me, but you'll be happier if you don't know."

Bessie felt that whatever Dolly might try to do to the other girls would serve them right, but she was worried about her chum. And when Dolly slipped off by herself after dinner, Bessie determined that she would not let her chum run any risks alone, even if she was not a sharer of Dolly's secret.

It was not a hard matter to trace Dolly, even though Bessie let her have a good start before she followed. She knew that any plan Dolly had must involve going to the other camp, and she hid herself, moving carefully so as to avoid detection, in a place that commanded the approach. And in a very short time she heard Dolly coming and saw that she was carrying a large basket with the utmost care.

CHAPTER XIV

Bessie stole along silently behind Dolly. She wanted very much to say something, but she was afraid of what might happen if she let Dolly know that she was spying on her. And she had made up her mind, anyhow, that she would do more harm than good by interfering at this time.

Whatever it was she was doing might be wrong, but, after all, she had a good deal of provocation, and she had been far more patient already than anyone who knew her would have expected her to be.

"I bet they're just trying to work her up to trying to get even," Bessie reflected to herself. "Gladys Cooper knows her, so she must know what a temper Dolly has, and she must be surprised to think that she hasn't managed to arouse her yet."

That thought made Bessie gladder than ever

that she had decided to follow Dolly. While she was not in the plot herself, she meant to be in it if Dolly got into trouble, or if, as Bessie half feared, it turned out that her chum was walking into a trap. Moreover, she was entirely ready to take her share of the blame, if there was to be any blame, and to let others believe that she had shared Dolly's secret from the first and had deliberately taken part in the plot.

Dolly's movements were puzzling. Bessie had expected her to go to the back of the camp, and when she heard laughter and the sound of loud talking coming from the boathouse, which was, of course, on the very shore of the lake, Bessie breathed a sigh of relief, since it seemed to her that the fact that the other girls were there would greatly increase Dolly's chance of escaping detection.

But instead of taking advantage of what Bessie regarded as a great piece of luck, Dolly paused to listen to the sounds from the boathouse, and then turned calmly and walked in its direction.

For a moment an unworthy suspicion crossed Bessie's mind.

"I wonder if she can be going to see them—to make up with them?" Bessie asked herself.

But she answered her own question with an emphatic no almost as soon as she had asked it. Dolly's anger the night before and that afternoon had not been feigned.

As she neared the boathouse, Dolly moved very cautiously. Even though she could see her, Bessie could not hear her, and she even had difficulty in following Dolly's movements, for she had put on a dark coat, and was an inconspicuous object in the darkness.

From the boathouse there now came the sound of music; a phonograph had been started, and it was plain from the shuffling of feet that the girls inside were dancing. Dolly crept closer and closer, until she reached one of the windows. Even as she did it a sharp, shrill voice cried out, and Bessie saw someone rush toward her from the darkness of a clump of trees near the boathouse. It

was a trap, after all! Bessie rushed forward, but
before she had taken more than a couple of steps,
and before, indeed, her assailant could reach her,
Dolly had accomplished her purpose.

Still running, Bessie saw her lift the basket she
carried, and throw it point-blank through the window, first taking off the cover. And then the noise
of the phonograph, the shout of Dolly's assailant,
and all the noises about the place were drowned
in a chorus of shrill screams of terror from inside
the boathouse.

Bessie had never heard such a din. For the
life of her she could not guess what Dolly had done
to produce such an effect, and she did not stop
to try. For the girl who had seen Dolly and rushed
toward her, although too late to stop her, had
caught hold of Dolly and was struggling to hold
her.

Bessie rushed at her, however, and, so unex-
pected was her coming, that the other girl let
go of Dolly and turned to grapple with the rescuer.
That was just what Bessie wanted. With a quick,

twisting motion she slipped out of the other girl's grip, and the next moment she was running as hard as she could to the back of the camp, where, if she could only get a good start, she would find herself in thick woods and so safe from pursuit.

She knew Dolly had recognized her at once. But neither had called the other's name, since that would enable whoever heard them to know which of the Camp Fire Girls was responsible for this sudden attack.

As she ran Bessie could hear Dolly in front of her, and she knew that Dolly must be able to hear her. Otherwise she was sure her chum would have turned back to rescue her. Behind her the screams of the frightened girls from the boat-house were still rising, but when Bessie stopped in ten minutes, she could hear no signs of pursuit.

"Dolly!' she cried. "It's all right to stop now. They're not chasing us any more."

Dolly stopped and waited for her, and when she came up Bessie saw at once that Dolly was angry —and at her.

"Much good it did you to try to stop me, didn't it?" said Dolly, viciously. "You got there too late!"

"I didn't try to stop you, and I was right behind you all the time!" said Bessie, angrily. "I was behind you so that if you got into any trouble I'd be there to help you—and I was. You're very grateful, aren't you?"

"Oh, Bessie, I am sorry! I might have known you wouldn't do anything sneaky. And you certainly did help me! I was going to thank you for that anyhow, as soon as I'd scolded you. But I knew you didn't want to try to get even with them, and I supposed, of course, that you were there to stop me."

Suddenly she began to laugh, and sat down weakly on the ground.

"Did you hear them yell?" she gasped. "Listen to them! They're still at it!"

"Whatever did you do to them, Dolly? I never heard such a noise in my life! You'd think they really had something to be afraid of."

"Yes, wouldn't you? Instead of just a basket full of poor, innocent little mice that were a lot more frightened than they were!"

"Dolly Ransom!" gasped Bessie. "Do you mean to say that is what you did?"

Bessie tried hard to be shocked, but the fun of it overcame her of a sudden, and she joined Dolly on the ground, while they clung to one another and rocked with laughter.

"I wasn't able to stop and watch them. That's all I'm sorry for now," said Dolly, weakly. "But hearing them was pretty nearly as fine, wasn't it?"

"Never heard of such a thing to do!" panted Bessie. "However did you manage it, Dolly? Where did you get the mice?"

"Promise not to tell, Bessie? I can't get anyone else into trouble, you know."

Bessie nodded.

"It was the guide—the Worcester's guide. He's just as mad at them as we are. It seems they've bothered him a lot, anyhow, and he didn't like them even before we came. He suggested the

whole thing, and he was willing to do it. But I
told him it was our quarrel, and that it was up to
one of us to do it if he would get the mice. So he
did, and put them in that basket for me. The rest
of it was easy.''

"They'll be perfectly wild, Dolly. I bet they'll
be over at the camp complaining when we get
back.''

"Let them complain! It won't do them much
good! Miss Eleanor is going to give me beans
for doing it, but she won't let them know it! I
know her, and she won't really be half as angry
as she'll pretend to be.''

"It was a wild thing to do, Dolly.''

"I suppose it was, but did you think I was going
to let Gladys Cooper tell all over town how they
treated us? She'll have something to tell this
time.''

"Well, you got even, Dolly. There's no doubt
of that. We'd better hurry back now, don't you
think? They're quieter down there.''

"I'm going to tell Miss Eleanor what I did just

as soon as I see her," said Dolly. "She'd find out that it happened sooner or later, and I'm not ashamed of having done it, either. I'd do the same thing to-morrow if I had as good a reason!"

And, sure enough, as soon as they reached the camp, Dolly marched up to Miss Eleanor, who was sitting by herself on the porch, and told her the whole story.

"And was Bessie in this too?" asked Eleanor, trying to look stern, but failing.

"No, she was not. She didn't know what I was going to do at all. She just followed to see that I didn't get into any trouble. And I'd have been caught if she hadn't been there."

"I—I'm sorry you did it, Dolly," said Eleanor, almost hysterically. She was trying to suppress the laughter that she was shaking with, but it was hard work. "Still, I don't believe I'll scold you very much. Now you've got even with them for all the things they've done—more than even, if the screams I heard mean anything. We didn't know what was up."

"Not exactly *what* was up," said Margery, who had overheard part of the conversation, "but we knew *who* was up as soon as we found you were gone, Dolly."

Margery looked at Miss Eleanor, then she choked, and left the porch hurriedly. And the next moment roars of laughter came from the other girls, as Margery told them the story.

"But I'm glad you've told me all about it, Dolly," said Eleanor. "I don't mind saying that I think you had a good deal of excuse—but do try to let things work out by themselves after this. The chances are you've only made them hate us more than ever, and they will feel that it's a point of honor now to get even with us for this. All the girls will have to suffer for what you did."

Even as she spoke, Bessie saw two or three figures approaching from the direction of the other camp, and a shrill voice was raised.

"There she is, Miss Brown. She's the one who's supposed to look after them."

Gladys Cooper was the speaker, but as soon as

she saw Eleanor look around she dropped back, leaving a woman whose manner was timid and nervous, and whose voice showed that she had little spirit, to advance alone.

"Miss Mercer?" she said, inquiringly, to Eleanor. "I am Miss Brown, and I have been left in charge of Miss Halsted's Camp this summer while she is away. She is ill. I am one of the teachers in her school—"

"Sit down, Miss Brown," said Eleanor, kindly. One look at poor Miss Brown explained the conduct of the girls in her care. She was one of those timid, nervous women who can never be expected to control anyone, much less a group of healthy, mischievous girls in need of a strong, restraining hand.

"I'm—really very sorry—I don't like—but I feel it is my duty—to speak to you, Miss Mercer," stammered Miss Brown. "The fact is—the young ladies seem to think it was one of your Camp Fire Girls who let loose a—number of mice in our boathouse this evening."

"I'm afraid it was, Miss Brown," said Eleanor, gravely. "And I need hardly say that I regret it. I naturally do not approve of anything of the sort. But your girls have themselves to blame to a certain extent."

"Why, I don't see how that can be!" said Miss Brown, looking bewildered.

"Now, Miss Brown, honestly, and just between us, haven't they made your life a burden for you ever since you've been here with them alone? Let me tell you what they've done since we've been here."

And calmly and without anger, Eleanor told the teacher of the various methods of making themselves unpleasant that the girls in the camp had adopted since the coming of the Camp Fire Girls. She raised her voice purposely when she came to the end.

"Now, mind, I don't approve of this joke with the mice," she said. "But I do think it would be more plucky if your girls, after starting all the trouble and making themselves as hateful as they possibly could, had kept quiet when the tables were turned. When they worried us, we didn't go over to make a complaint about them. I must say I am disappointed in those of your girls whom I happen to know, like Gladys Cooper. I thought she was a lady.''

There was a furious cry from the darkness beyond the porch, and the next instant Gladys herself was in front of Eleanor, with tears of rage in her eyes.

''You shan't say I'm not a lady!'' she cried. ''I don't care if you are Miss Mercer! We don't want your horrid charity girls up here, and we tried to make them understand it—''

''Stop!'' said Eleanor, sternly. ''Listen to me, Gladys! I like your mother, and I'm sorry to see you acting in such a way. What do you mean by charity girls?''

''They haven't got the money to come up here,'' stammered Gladys.

''It hasn't been given to them, if you mean that,'' said Eleanor. ''We don't believe in idle, useless girls in the Camp Fire. And every girl here, even those like Dolly Ransom, who could have got the money at home very easily, have earned all their expenses for this vacation, except two who didn't have time, and are here as my guests. Don't talk about charity. They have a better right to be here than you have. Now go away, and if you don't want to have unpleasant things happen to you, don't do unpleasant things to other people.''

Quite cowed by the sudden anger in Eleanor's voice, Gladys didn't hesitate. And Miss Brown, before she left the porch, looked wistfully at Eleanor.

''I wish I had your courage, my dear,'' she whispered. ''That served Gladys right, but if I spoke so to her, I should lose my position.''

''Well, I suppose it wasn't a nice thing to do,'' said Dolly, as she and Bessie prepared for bed that night. ''But I really do think we won't have any more trouble. I think Gladys and the rest of them have learned a lesson.''

"I hope so, Dolly," said Bessie. "I wouldn't have done it myself, but I really am beginning to think that maybe it was the best thing that could have happened. Thunderstorms clear the air sometimes; perhaps this will have the same effect."

It was well after midnight when the girls were awakened by loud knocking below.

"Oh, that's some trick of theirs," said Dolly, sleepily, and turned over again.

But a few minutes later Eleanor's voice, calling them, took them downstairs in a hurry. They found her talking to Miss Brown, who was in tears.

"Girls," said Eleanor, "Gladys Cooper and another girl are lost, and they must be out on the mountain. It's turned very cold. Shall we help find them? We haven't been friends, but remember what Wo-he-lo means!"

CHAPTER XV

There wasn't a single dissenting voice. Once they knew what was required, the girls rushed at once to their rooms to dress, and within ten minutes they were all assembled on the porch. Mingled with them were most of the girls from Miss Halsted's camp, thoroughly frightened and much distressed, and evidently entirely forgetful of the trouble that had existed as late as that evening between the two camps.

"Now, I'll tell you very quickly what the situation is," said Eleanor. "Don't mind asking questions, but make them short. It seems that some of the other girls over there were angry at Gladys when they got back there after Miss Brown came here to see me. And they told her she had been wrong in setting them against us."

"I knew she was the one who had done it!" Dolly whispered to Bessie.

233

"She and one other girl, Marcia Bates, were great chums, and they got angry. They said they wouldn't stay to be abused—isn't that right, Miss Brown?—and they decided to go for a walk in the woods back of the lake here."

"They've often done it before," said Miss Brown. "I thought it was all right and they would have gone, anyhow, even if I'd told them not to do it."

"When they started," Eleanor went on, "the moon was up, and there were plenty of stars, so that they should have been able to find their way back easily, guided by the moon or by the Big Bear—the Dipper. But it's clouded up since then and it's begun to rain. The wind has changed, too, and they might easily have lost themselves."

"Wouldn't they be on a regular trail?" asked Margery Burton.

"There aren't any regular trails back here," spoke up one of the girls from the Halsted camp. "There are just a lot of little paths that criss-cross back and forth, and keep on getting mixed

up. It's hard enough to find your way in day-
light.''

''They have sent for guides from the big hotel
at the head of the lake,'' said Eleanor. ''They
will get here as soon as they can, and a few men
are out searching already. But I think the best
thing for us to do is to organize a regular patrol.
We'll beat up the mountain quickly, and pretty
well together, in a long line, so that there won't
be more than a hundred feet between any two of
us. Then when we get to the ridge about half way
up we'll start back, and cover the ground more
carefully, if we haven't found them.''

''Why won't we go beyond the ridge?'' asked
Dolly.

''We'll leave that part to the men. I think myself that it's most unlikely they would go beyond
that. I've had our guides here make up a whole
lot of resinous torches. They'll burn very
brightly, and for a long time, and each of us will
take as many as she can carry, about fifteen or
twenty.

"And I've made up a lot of little first-aid pack-
ages, in case one of the girls is hurt, or has twisted
her ankle. That may be the reason they're out so
late. When we start to come back we'll break up
in twos, and each pair will go back and forth, instead of coming straight down, so that we'll cover
the whole side of the mountain."

"How shall we know if we find them?" asked
Bessie. "I mean how will the others know?"

"I've got one horn for every two of us," said
Eleanor. "One toot won't mean anything, just
that we're keeping in touch. But whoever finds
them is to blow five or six times, very close together. It's very still in the woods, and a signal
like that can be heard even when you're· a long
way from it."

"Can't some of us go and help, Miss Mercer?"
asked one of the Halsted girls, the one, incident-
ally, who had been the ruling spirit in the trick
to spoil the pleasures of swimming for the Camp
Fire Girls. .

"I think you better stay at home, and get a lot

of good hot coffee or broth or something ready for them when they get back,'' said Eleanor. ''They'll need something of the sort, I can promise you. And really, I'm afraid you'd be rather useless in the woods. Our girls, you see, have to be able to find their way pretty well. You'll be more useful at home.''

''I don't expect to find them on the way up,'' said Eleanor, as they started. ''We might, of course, but we'll look better coming back, and it's then that I think we'll have the best chance. Come on, now! Shout every little while.''

The night was pitch black now. A fine mist of rain was falling and threatening to become a steady downpour. It was a bad night for anyone, even those who were hardened, to be out in the woods without shelter or special covering, and it was about as bad as it could be for girls who were not at all used to even the slightest exposure.

Eleanor's face was very grave, and she looked exceedingly worried as she crossed back and forth in front of the line of Camp Fire Girls, lifting her own voice in shouts to the lost ones, and giving hints here and there for the more important home-ward journey.

The trip up the mountain produced no results. The rain was falling more heavily, and, moreover, the wind was rising. It blew hard through the trees and the silence of the woods that Eleanor had spoken of was a thing of the past. The wind sighed and groaned, and Eleanor grew more and more worried.

"We've got to search just as carefully as we can," she said. "We mustn't leave any part of this ground uncovered. With all the noise the wind is making, we might easily pass within a few feet of them and shout at the top of our lungs without them hearing us. It is going to be even harder to find them than I feared, but we have just got to do the best we can."

At the top of the ridge of which she had spoken, Eleanor marshalled her forces. She told them off two by two, and Bessie and Dolly were assigned to work together.

"I'm going to cover the whole ground, and keep in touch with all of you," she said. "Keep blowing your horns, there's more chance that they will be heard. You all have your pocket compasses and plenty of matches, haven't you? I don't want any of my own girls to be lost."

"All right," she said, when they had all answered. "Now I want each of you to take a strip about six yards wide as we go down, and just walk back and forth across it. If you come to any gullies or holes where they might have fallen down be particularly careful. Light your torches, and look into them. Don't pay attention to the paths or trails, just cover the ground."

"Oh, I do hope we can find them!" said Bessie, as they started. "I'd hate to think of their being out here all night on a night like this."

"Yes, and in a way it's really my fault," said Dolly, remorsefully.

"Why, Dolly, how can you think that?"

"It was because Gladys quarrelled with the rest of them that she went out. And if I hadn't thrown

those mice in at them there wouldn't have been
any quarrel. Don't you see?"

"I think it's silly to blame yourself, though,
Dolly. She might have gone out just the same,
anyhow."

"Well, I'll never forgive myself if anything
happens to them, Bessie. I might have kept my
temper, the way you and Margery did. They
didn't do any more to me than they did to the rest
of you. Oh, I am sorry, and I am going to try to
control myself better after this."

Then they went on in silence for a time. Bessie
felt sorry for Dolly, and she really did think that
Dolly's conscience, now that it was beginning to
awaken, was doing more than its share. It was
unlike the care-free Dolly to worry about anything
she had done, but it was like her, too, to accuse
herself unsparingly once she began to realize that
she might possibly be in the wrong. It was Dolly's
old misfortune that was grieving her now; her
inability to forecast consequences before they came
along to confound her.

For a long time they had no results, and the blowing of horns and the occasional flash of a torch between the trees showed them that the others were meeting with no better success. Sometimes, too, Eleanor joined them for a moment. She could tell them nothing, and they continued to search with unabated vigor.

"Look, Bessie!" said Dolly, suddenly. She had lighted a torch to explore a gully a few moments before, and it was still burning brightly. Now it showed them the opening of what looked like a cave, black and dismal looking.

"Why, do you think they might be in there?" asked Bessie. "I'll blow my horn in the mouth. They'd hear that, and come out."

But blow as hard as she would, there was no answer. She turned away in disappointment.

"I'm afraid they're not there," she said.

"I'm going in to find out," said Dolly, suddenly. "They might not have heard us. You can't tell what that horn would sound like in there; it might not make any noise at all."

4—C16

"Oh, I don't believe they're in there," said Bessie. "And I think it might be dangerous. There might be snakes there, or a hole you would fall into, Dolly."

"I don't care! This is all my fault, and I'm going!"

And without another word, she plunged into the dark entrance. Bessie tried to call her back, but Dolly paid no heed. And in a moment, first leaving behind signs of their having gone in, Bessie followed her, lighting another torch. She had not gone far when she heard a happy cry from Dolly.

"Here they are! I've found them!" Dolly shouted. "They're sound asleep, and I don't believe there's a thing the matter with them!"

Nor was there. Both the lost girls slept soundly, and when Gladys finally woke up, blinking at the light of the torches, she looked indignantly at Dolly.

"You're a sneak, Dolly Ransom!" she said. "I should think you would want to stay with your own sort of people—"

But Dolly was too happy at finding the pair of strays to care what Gladys said to her.

"Oh, come off, Gladys!" she said. "I suppose you don't know that you're lost, and that half the people around the lake are out looking for you? Come on! You'll catch a frightful cold lying here with those thin dresses on. Hurry, now!"

And finally she managed to arouse them enough to make them understand the situation. Even then, however, Gladys was sullen.

"That's that silly old Miss Brown," she said. "It's just like her to go running off to your crowd for help, Dolly. I suppose we ought to be grateful, but we'd have been all right there until morning."

Dolly didn't care to argue the matter. Her one thought now was to get outside of the cave and send out by means of the horns the glad news that the lost ones were found. In a few moments she and Bessie, blowing with all their might, announced the good tidings.

"Now you two will just walk as fast as you can,

so that you can get into bed and have something warm inside of you. I'll be pretty mad if you get pneumonia and die after all the trouble we've taken to save you!'' she said, laughing.

Gladys wasn't in any mood, it seemed, to appreciate a joke. As a matter of fact, both she and Marcia Bates had awakened stiff from the cold, and though she wouldn't admit it she was very glad of the prospect of a warm and comfortable bed.

And when the searchers and the rescued ones reached the Halsted Camp, Gladys wasn't left long in doubt as to the fate of the vendetta she had declared against the Camp Fire Girls. For, even while she was being put to bed, she could hear the cheers that were being given by her own chums for the girls she had tried to make them despise.

''Oh, Miss Mercer, I think you and the Camp Fire Girls are splendid!'' said Emily Turner, the big girl who had been the ringleader of the tricks with the motor boat. ''You're going to stay here quite a while, aren't you?''

"No," said Eleanor, regretfully. "It was only the fire that made us stay here as long as we have. Now this wind and rain have ended that, and we'll go on as soon as the storm is over; day after to-morrow, if it clears up to-morrow, so that it will be dry when we start."

"Well, I hope we'll see you again—all of you," said Emily. "Come on, girls, let's give the school cheer for the Manasquan Camp Fire!"

They gave it with a will and then Dolly sprang to her feet.

"Now, then, the Wo-he-lo cheer!" she called.

They sang it happily, and then, as they moved toward their own camp, their voices rose in the good-night song of the Camp Fire: *Lay me to sleep in sheltering flame.*

"I believe Miss Eleanor was right, after all," said Bessie. "Those girls really like us now."

"All but Gladys Cooper," said Dolly. "But then she doesn't know any better. And she'll learn."

John Newbery Series

Early in the 18th century John Newbery was born in a little Berkshire village in England, and became a bookman in the old St. Paul's churchyard.

It was he who first believed children needed books of their own, and he set about to supply that need. Many of the old stories, quaint jingles and nursery rhymes we have today are due to him. It is therefore peculiarly fitting this series, comprising the best written for childhood, should bear his name.

THE PIED PIPER OF HAMELIN— *Robert Browning*

THE KING OF THE GOLDEN RIVER— *John Ruskin*

MONI, THE GOAT BOY—*Johanna Spyri*

FAIRY TALE GIANTS

FAIRY TALE PRINCES

FAIRY TALE PRINCESSES

A DOG OF FLANDERS—*Louisa de la Ramee (Ouida)*

THE LEGEND OF SLEEPY HOLLOW— *Washington Irving*

RIP VAN WINKLE—*Washington Irving*

THE NURNBERG STOVE—*Louisa de la Ramee (Ouida)*

THE ADVENTURES OF A BROWNIE— *Miss Mulock*

CHILD VERSES—*Eugene Field*

These books are well bound in cloth, are profusely illustrated, have a colored frontispiece and a colored jacket, and contain 92 pages each.

THE SAALFIELD PUBLISHING CO.
AKRON, OHIO